"The Only Reason I Slept With Your Brother Was Because Of You," Helene said softly.

"What do you mean?" Chris murmured.

"I loved Martin, I know I did. But there are all types of love, and I was worried that the gratitude I felt for him was misleading me. I thought if I slept with him it would clear up the confusion."

Chris seemed to be holding his breath. "Did it?"

Helene closed her eyes. "It...didn't help. Martin was very sweet, but it wasn't..."

"Like it is with us," he finished.

"Yes," she said in a small voice.

Chris reached her side in two strides and swept her greedily into his arms.

"Wait," she pleaded. "We have to think—"

"No," he muttered, kissing the side of her neck. "There's been too much damn thinking going on around here." His lips traveled up to her cheek and found her mouth. Helene responded hungrily, giving up, losing herself....

Dear Reader,

You know, there are some months here at Silhouette Desire that I feel are simply perfect! Naturally, I think each and every Desire book is just wonderful, but occasionally the entire lineup is so special I have to mention each book separately.

Let's start with *Hazards of the Heart* by Dixie Browning. This talented author has been writing for the line since nearly the very beginning—over ten years ago! Still, it's hard for me to believe that this is her *fiftieth* Silhouette book. *Hazards of the Heart* is highlighted as our *Man of the Month,* and it also contains a special letter from Dixie to you, her loyal readers.

Joan Johnston is fast becoming a favorite, but if you haven't yet experienced her sexy western-flavored stories, please give her a try! *The Rancher and the Runaway Bride* is the first of her new series, *Hawk's Way,* which takes place—mostly—on a Texas ranch. The stories concern the lives—and new loves—of the two Whitelaw brothers and their sassy sister.

A book from Lass Small is always a delight, and this time around we have *A Disruptive Influence.* What—or *who?*— is this disruptive influence? Why, read and find out.

As far as I'm concerned, Nancy Martin has been too long from the list, therefore I'm *thrilled* with *Good Golly, Miss Molly.* Doreen Owens Malek is another author we just don't see enough of, so I'm equally excited about *The Harder They Fall.* And I love Lucy Gordon's emotional writing style. If you're also a fan, don't miss *Married in Haste.*

Six spectacular books by six dynamite authors. Can you ask for anything more?

Until next month, happy reading!

Lucia Macro
Senior Editor

DOREEN OWENS MALEK
THE HARDER THEY FALL

SILHOUETTE *Desire*®

™ Published by Silhouette Books New York

America's Publisher of Contemporary Romance

SILHOUETTE BOOKS
300 East 42nd St., New York, N.Y. 10017

THE HARDER THEY FALL

Copyright © 1993 by Doreen Owens Malek

ISBN: 0-373-05778-4

First Silhouette Books printing April 1993

DOREEN OWENS MALEK

is a former attorney who decided on her current career when she sold her fledgling novel to the first editor who read it. Since then, she has gained recognition for her writing, winning honors from *Romantic Times* magazine and the coveted Golden Medallion award. She has traveled extensively throughout Europe, but it was in her home state of New Jersey that she met and married her college sweetheart. They now live in their home in Pennsylvania.

One

"So tell me more about your brother," Helene said, watching as Martin set her suitcase on the bed and then looked briskly around the room, surveying it.

"This guest room hasn't changed at all since I was last here," he observed. "Same rug and bedspread. I don't think Chris goes in much for interior decoration."

"Martin?" Helene prompted.

"Yes?" he said, glancing at her.

"Your brother. I've come all the way out here to Wyoming to meet him and what you've said about the man so far could be printed on a postage stamp."

Martin grinned. "Well, he'll be back from the branding at five, then you can see for yourself."

Helene sighed. "You're being evasive."

"Lawyer's habit, Miss Danforth," Martin replied, leaning forward to kiss her on the forehead. "If you're going to marry me and become Mrs. Murdock you'll have to get used to it."

"Be that as it may, I think I should have a little preparation before I meet him. Is he anything like you?"

Martin sat on the edge of the bed and smiled. "No."

"Your father?"

Martin grinned. "Exactly like my father. Not in looks, but Chris has the same stubbornness and pride and iron will. When he first showed up here we didn't have to guess whether he was really a member of the family, he had my dad's personality to a *T.*"

"When did he come here?"

"When he was fifteen. His mother had just died, as I've already told you. He was running wild, a chip on his shoulder the size of Mount Everest and all alone in the world. He'd really been alone before that, I guess. His mother had always been more devoted to the bottle than to him. Anyway, he had quite a local reputation, just kid stuff really, fighting and raising hell and getting thrown out of schools." He grinned. "He was going to make it clear that he didn't need anybody, you know? Scared stiff, of course, but he would have been shot rather than show it."

"I gather you won him over," Helene said gently.

"Oh, it took a while. He had no experience of... kindness. He needed some time to get used to it. I remember once when he'd been arrested for mouthing off to some cop and they were holding him down at the station. It was nothing serious, but his attitude was not helping him get released. A smart-aleck kid—you can appreciate how the cops loved him."

Helene nodded.

"I came to the police station to bail him out and you should have seen the look on his face when he spotted me. It was just after he had come to live with us and it was obvious to me that he hadn't expected anybody to help him. After all, no one ever had. I was fresh out of law school and didn't really know what I was doing anyway, but just my showing up made a great impression on him. He was different after that—he would listen to me instead of flying off the handle the moment I tried to talk to him."

"And your father?"

"Oh, Dad took to him right away. Chris was everything I wasn't—bold and handsome, physically brave, close to fearless, in fact. And once he calmed down and gave us a chance he was just like an animal who'd been mistreated but then found a loving home. All that anger turned into devotion." Martin swallowed hard. "He just idolized my dad and my father felt he had to make up for lost time, so they became very close."

"But weren't you jealous?" Helene asked.

Martin laughed. "Oh, how could I be? He became my champion! You know that saying: 'He's not heavy, he's my brother.' That's Chris. Even today he sees himself as my protector."

"I thought the older brother was supposed to protect the younger one," Helene said, chuckling.

"Tell him that. As far as he's concerned, he's Mr. Worldly Wise and I'm the chump who'll give away his socks if he's not watched."

"Isn't that a bit much? No one has felt your generosity more than I have, but even I know you're not naive."

"I can see that you'll get along famously with Chris," Martin said, rising. "I can't wait for you to meet him. Now why don't you shower and change, maybe have a rest, while I go out and find my brother. I want to surprise him, since he's not expecting us until tomorrow morning. I won't be gone long."

Before Helene could reply he was through the door and she heard his footsteps fading down the hall. She wandered over to the skirted vanity table and sat down, studying her reflection in the glass.

She looked tired, and it was no surprise. So much had happened in the past few months that she sometimes wondered how she had been able to deal with it all.

First had come her father's disgrace, through which she had met Martin. James Danforth had declared bankruptcy at the beginning of the year and Martin was the attorney handling the proceeding. During the auditor's examination of her father's complicated financial records, it emerged that he had been embezzling from his company for some time. Unable to endure the thought of his forthcoming exposure, he had killed himself in April. Helene's mother, always sheltered and delicate, could not handle the scandal and humiliation and had withdrawn into a shadow world, leaving her other child, Helene's ten year old sister, to fend for herself. The house and property were sold to make a court ordered restitution, leaving the family homeless and virtually destitute, a situation Helene could not hope to remedy by herself on her teacher's salary. Things had looked very bleak.

Through it all, Martin, an old friend of James Danforth's, had been a rock to cling to while dangerous waters swirled around the Danforth family. Martin had started his law firm with client recommendations from the senior Danforth, and even when Helene's father had become a pariah Martin had not abandoned his old friend's wife and children. He had been so helpful, in fact, that Helene found herself leaning on him, perhaps a lot more than she should have. He had been so kind and caring that she should not have been shocked when he asked her to marry him.

Helene rose and walked to the window, looking out across the expanse of the Murdock family ranch spread beneath her. At first she had refused Martin's proposal, unsure of her own feelings. She respected and admired him, and she cared deeply for him, but she was confused and afraid that she would be doing him a disservice if she accepted him. But Martin had persisted, offering to take care of her family anyway, even if she didn't marry him. When Helene protested that she couldn't allow him to do that, he had said that he was repaying a debt to her father and had ignored her objections. His relentless kindness, his gentleness with her devastated mother and bewildered sister had worn down her resistance. Over Helene's objections he had established a trust for the surviving Danforths and installed them in a condominium owned by his firm. He had handled all the legal proceedings with a minimum of fuss for the family and generally had made himself indispensable. He was the most wonderful man she had ever known, and two weeks earlier Helene had finally agreed to marry him.

She sighed heavily. Was something missing? she wondered. She had never been in love, so she had no way of judging. She cared for Martin and she wanted to make him happy. Helene bit her lip as she watched a ranch hand cross the lawn beneath her, heading for the stables with a bridle in his hand. She would try very hard to be worthy of Martin.

She wandered into the adjoining bathroom and turned on the taps for a bath. The plane flight out from New Jersey to Wyoming had been rocky and she felt the need for a long, relaxing soak before she met Martin's brother.

Chris ran the Homestead, the ranch both men had inherited from their father. Martin had explained some time ago that he had never had any interest in ranching, so after graduating from law school in New York he had remained in the East and made a career there. Helene had been startled then to learn that Christopher, the younger brother, was illegitimate. He had gone unacknowledged by his father for more than half his life, since the elder Murdock did not know he existed. Chris had not found out who his father was until his mother had died and her will revealed his parentage. Chris was fifteen by then, and thus had the difficult entrance into the family Martin had just described.

Helene had been fascinated to discover that solid, dependable Martin had such a skeleton in his family closet. Since the one occasion on which he had discussed his half brother he had refused to say anything more, always deflecting her questions lightly but firmly until today. It was clear that Martin wanted Chris to be judged entirely for himself.

Helene unbuttoned her blouse, bending to sample the temperature of the water. She admired Martin's attempt to be fair, but she felt at a disadvantage. She had been ushered West to meet a complete stranger, one whose opinion was obviously important to Martin, and she had very little to prepare her for encountering her fiancé's only relative. She frowned as she discarded the rest of her clothes.

She was anxious to be liked, for Martin's sake, but she wasn't sure how to accomplish that. She could only be herself and hope for the best. She stepped into the tub and turned off the taps.

Chris Murdock wiped his streaming face with a towel and lifted his discarded shirt from the railing at his left.

"That's enough for today, Sam," he said to the leather-skinned ranch hand who was working at his side. "We'll finish the rest of them tomorrow."

Sam nodded and gestured for the remainder of the bawling calves to be herded back into the pen. Two other hands removed the steaming branding irons from the fire and put them on a rack to cool.

Chris glanced up at the setting sun, ruffling his damp hair with the towel.

"Plenty warm for June," Sam observed.

Chris nodded. It would be a long, hot summer.

"It will cool off tonight and be chilly, always does this time of year. Is your brother arriving tomorrow with his girl?" Sam said.

Chris nodded again. Sam noticed the darkening of his expression and thought it best not to pursue the subject.

"I'm going up to the house," Chris said shortly, tossing the towel onto a pile of discarded burlap feed sacks and tying his shirt around his waist. He strode out of the paddock and onto the path that led up to the sprawling redwood ranch his father had built more than thirty years earlier. As he walked he thought about his coming encounter with Martin's future bride.

What a fiasco that was going to be. Some chippy had attached herself to his pushover of a brother and he was supposed to rejoice about it. Martin, well off at forty, a whiz at business but never a ladies' man, was the perfect patsy for a scheming younger woman. Everything Chris had heard about this girl, from her criminally inclined father to her dependent mother and sister, had convinced him that she was using his sympathetic, sweet-natured sibling. He himself had ben-

efited from Martin's goodness—who else would have
understood the surly teenager who had surfaced as his
half brother, resenting the life of privilege Martin had
led while he had been fatherless and poor. Martin
never felt supplanted by the hellion upstart his father
had grown to adore, and Chris had never forgotten his
brother's generosity. And he was damned if he was
going to stand by and let some gold digger young
enough to be Martin's daughter take advantage of it.
Martin seemed certain that once Chris met Helene his
doubts would vanish, but Chris was not so sure. He
might be younger than Martin but he knew a hell of a
lot more about women and this smelled like a setup to
him.

He rounded the corner of the porch and went to the
back pump to rinse off before entering the house.

Helene stood in the empty kitchen wondering where
Martin was. He had been gone for almost two hours
and it was getting on toward dinnertime. She found a
copper kettle sitting on the range, filled it at the sink
and set it on to boil. She was fidgeting around looking for tea bags when the back door opened and a man
strode through it, stopping short when he saw her.

They stared at one another, both of them surprised
into silence.

The first impression Helene had was of size; she was
tall herself, but this man topped her by several inches.
He was dark, with damp and tousled raven hair and
olive skin kissed by the sun. His sherry brown eyes

narrowed as he examined her, their long lashes matted with moisture. He was naked to the waist, his shoulders broad and spattered with freckles, his upper arms muscular. Helene's gaze traveled to the black hair spreading over his chest and disappearing in a line under his belt. She looked away deliberately, her face flushing.

"So, who are you?" he finally said, his low voice deep and resonant.

"I'm...I'm Helene," she stuttered, forcing herself to meet his eyes directly.

"The fiancée?" he said skeptically, folding his arms. "Aren't you a little early?"

"Yes. And yes. I've just been waiting for Martin— he should have been back by now..." she said helplessly.

"I'm Chris. You know, the brother?" he said dryly, stepping forward and extending his hand.

Helene clasped it, feeling a slight shock as her fingers slipped into his callused palm.

"I'm sorry I wasn't here to greet you," he said evenly. "I wasn't expecting you until tomorrow."

"Yes, we were able to get an earlier flight. There was a cancellation and Martin didn't see the sense of just hanging around the airport. Perhaps we should have called you, but there really wasn't any time...." Her voice trailed off as she realized that she was babbling. She pulled her hand back from his uncomfortably. Even though his words had been perfectly polite, she felt something amiss in him. He fairly radiated... what? Embarrassment? Dislike?

"Excuse me a moment," he said. "I'm not really fit company for a lady."

Was her imagination working overtime or did she sense a faint sneering emphasis on the last word?

"I'll be right back," he added, disappearing into the darkness of the house. Helene turned the gas jet off under the teakettle. When he returned his hair had been combed and he was wearing a deep red polo shirt that emphasized his dark good looks.

Helene could hardly believe that this was Martin's brother; there was no physical resemblance between the two men at all. Martin was stocky and blond, whereas this man was leaner, taller and Martin's opposite in coloring as well as build.

"Don't look much like Martin, do I?" he said, reading her thoughts. "Physically, he takes after the old man. I look like my mother, who was Spanish, and never married to our father, I might add."

She said nothing. His faintly sardonic air disturbed her.

"She was the maid, you know," he added in a mocking whisper, then grinned, displaying large white teeth.

"Martin told me about it," Helene replied, not knowing what else to say.

"Shocking, don't you think? Has he been unburdening himself of all the family secrets?" Chris inquired.

Helene was spared a reply by Martin's arrival. He came through the same door Chris had used and Helene was so relieved to see him she almost fell on his neck in greeting.

"There you are!" Martin said triumphantly to his brother, hugging Helene to his side. "I've been looking all over this place for you!" He released her and extended his hand to Chris, who seized it and then embraced him, thumping Martin on the back. Helene watched the two men, feeling a little misty at their obvious affection for one another.

"I see you've met Helene," Martin said.

"Yes," Chris replied, stepping back from his brother.

There was a silence.

"Isn't she beautiful?" Martin prompted eagerly, beaming at his fiancée.

"Very," Chris said quietly.

"I had come down here to wait for you and Chris found me," Helene said hurriedly, to change the subject.

"Good, good. I want you two to get along, you know," Martin said, still smiling broadly.

Chris looked at Helene and then away.

"Sorry to barge in like this, but we had the opportunity to get here a little sooner and we took it," Martin added. "You're probably not ready to feed us, Chris, so what do you say to a dinner on the town? I'm starving and I see that Maria has gone home for the day."

"Sure," Chris said.

They all stood awkwardly in the kitchen, glancing at one another uneasily.

"Well, let's get going," Martin said briskly. "My rental is parked out in front."

"Nothing doing," Chris retorted. "I'm driving."

"I'm not sure Helene is ready for that experience," Martin observed dryly.

"What does that mean?" Helene asked nervously.

"Chris used to drive race cars," Martin explained. "Sometimes he gets the public roads confused with a dirt track."

"I'll drive like a little old lady on her way to church," Chris said sarcastically.

"I'm relieved to hear it," Martin said.

They went out to Chris's car, which turned out to be a low-slung Italian sports car with a vestigial back seat, into which Martin climbed, insisting that Helene take the full front seat next to Chris. She got in as gracefully as possible, smoothing her skirt down over her knees carefully, then looked away in confusion when she saw Chris watching her. She stared straight ahead, extremely conscious of the man beside her, his muscular thighs encased in cord jeans, a large brown hand on the gear shift. When she stole another glance at him his expression was grim.

During the drive to the restaurant Martin kept up a running conversation with Chris about the ranch and local people. Helene had wondered about reservations, but once they got there she realized that Chris had an inside track. They were greeted like royalty and shown to a secluded table next to a niche containing a plaster statue of Don Quixote. The plush red carpeting and heavy carved furniture gave the room a Mediterranean feeling. Helene was seated in a padded leather chair with brass studs on the arms and given a menu printed in Spanish.

"Have you ever had this kind of food before?" Chris asked, as a waiter hovered in the background.

"No," Helene replied, glancing uneasily at Martin.

"Give it a chance, you'll like it," Martin said.

"Tres margaritas, por favor," Chris said to the waiter, who promptly vanished.

"Oh, nothing for me," Helene said, looking up from the menu.

"You don't drink?" Chris asked, arching one black brow.

"Not much."

"I guess I'll just have to drink yours, then," Chris offered, smiling at her lazily.

Helene felt the warmth creeping up her neck at his penetrating gaze and concentrated on shredding a roll.

"What do you recommend?" Martin asked his brother. "They've changed the menu since I was last here."

"Mussels in green sauce for an appetizer," Chris said.

Green sauce? Helene thought. She'd pass.

"And the *paella* is good," Chris added.

"What's that?" Helene asked.

"Saffron rice with a mixture of chicken and sausage, scallops and shrimp."

"All that?" she said, dismayed.

"Or you can have *arroz con pollo,*" Chris added. "That's always safe for the tourists."

Helene looked at him inquiringly.

"Chicken and rice," he explained.

"That sounds fine," she said, relieved.

"Not too foreign?" Chris suggested mildly.

Helene looked at Martin, who was watching the exchange between his fiancée and his brother intently.

"Helene has rather plain taste in food," Martin said.

"No continental restaurants in New Jersey?" Chris inquired.

"I haven't been able to afford them," she replied flatly.

"But of course you'll be able to soon, once you marry my brother," Chris said evenly. "So I guess you can consider this a foretaste of the good life."

Martin looked at him sharply.

"Margaritas," the waiter announced, depositing the drinks at each place on the table.

Chris picked his up and drained half of it in one swallow.

"So," he said to Helene as he put his glass down, "what's your job back East?"

"I teach first grade."

"Little kids?"

"Yes, they're around seven."

"I guess you'll be giving that up once you get married," Chris said, fiddling with the salt cellar on the table.

"No, I hadn't planned to do that," Helene replied.

"Why not? You won't need the money."

"I enjoy my job and that's reason enough to keep it," Helene said, rising. "Will you excuse me, please?"

"The ladies' room is to the right of the entrance," Martin said as she left the table. He waited until Helene was out of earshot and then said tightly to Chris, "Do you mind telling me what you're doing?"

"I don't know what you're talking about," Chris replied flatly, draining his drink.

"You're needling Helene," Martin said.

"I'm just asking her about her background, trying to make conversation," Chris replied mildly.

"Bull."

"Don't you want me to talk to her?"

"I don't want you to imply with your every word and gesture that she's after me for my money."

Chris stared back at him without replying.

"It may interest you to know that it has taken me months to get that woman to accept my proposal and if you keep treating her this way she may just change her mind," Martin said heatedly.

"I'm sure she required a lot of persuasion, what with her father dead, the family destitute and only her first-grade teacher's salary to bail them out," Chris said dryly.

"What is the matter with you?" Martin demanded. "I've wanted a home and a family for a long time and you certainly know that. I'm clearly old enough to make my own decisions. If this is the person I choose, you should welcome her. She's hardly a streetwalker, which is the way you've been acting."

"So you think a young, beautiful girl like that is marrying you because she's madly in love with you?" Chris countered.

"Oh, I see. I'm too old and stodgy to attract anyone like Helene for any reason except the stability I can provide, is that it?"

"I didn't say that," Chris said grimly, seizing Helene's margarita and downing a gulp of it.

Helene approached the table and the men fell silent. Shortly afterward the waiter took their order and the meal proceeded, in an atmosphere of palpable tension. By the time they left to return to the ranch Martin was making desperate small talk and Chris was replying in monosyllables. Helene had given up and stared out the window all the way back, ignoring the man driving the car beside her.

When they got back, Helene pleaded fatigue and retired to the guest room. Martin took the bedroom next to hers and Chris had the room at the end of the hall. Helene undressed quickly and got into bed, but she was unable to sleep. The evening kept replaying itself in her mind; she felt the dark eyes of Martin's brother on her as if he were with her at that moment. Why did he trouble her so much?

She finally got out of bed in frustration and paced around the room. Moonlight streamed across the bed and illuminated the ghostly shapes of the furniture.

She went into the adjoining bathroom and splashed water on her face, glancing in the mirror above the sink as she patted her cheeks dry. Her flaxen hair streamed over her shoulders and her blue eyes looked

huge and vague in her pale face. She closed her eyes
wearily and leaned against the door.

Why had Martin's brother taken such an instant
dislike to her? What had she done wrong? It was true
that she had arrived unexpectedly and he'd found her
prowling about his kitchen, but that had been explained. And why did she feel so odd when he looked
at her, as if she wanted to run away and yet were nailed
to the floor at the same time?

Helene sighed. Her mother was right, she thought
as she went back into the bedroom, she should have
dated more. Then maybe she would be better at handling men. But her shyness had been such that she had
preferred the company of her family and the books she
got from the library. Even in college she had chosen an
early childhood major because she knew she would
not be comfortable teaching older children. And now
here she was trying to win over Martin's obviously
hostile brother without the background or experience
to deal with him. She wished mightily that she were a
femme fatale; at least then she would not feel gauche
and helpless every time Chris looked at her. She was
comfortable with Martin, that was part of his attrac-
tion for her, and she had naturally expected to feel the
same way with his brother. The uneasiness with Chris
had come as a rude surprise and its aftermath was now
keeping her awake.

She remembered a sleep aid from childhood and
decided to go to the kitchen to heat some milk. She
padded barefoot down the hall in her cotton nightgown and slipped into the darkened kitchen, locating

a carton of milk in the refrigerator. She found a saucepan in the cupboard under the sink and heated the milk, pouring it into a glass and then tiptoeing past the living room. She was taking a sip of the hot drink when a deep voice said, "Why don't you join me?"

Helene started so violently that the milk slopped from the glass and spattered her bare feet. She looked over her shoulder and realized that the deep chair fronting the fireplace was occupied. Its back was so high that she had not seen Chris sitting there. He was staring into a dying blaze in the grate, swirling an inch of amber liquid in a glass. As she walked across the parquet floor toward him he saluted her with the tumbler and said. "Can't sleep?"

"No," she replied, standing awkwardly in front of him, holding her milk before her as if it were a chalice.

"Me neither," he said. "Must be the mussels, they have a tendency to come back and haunt you."

"I didn't eat any mussels."

"That's right. In fact, you didn't eat much of anything. Did I spoil your appetite?"

"I . . . wasn't very hungry."

"Ah. So polite. Don't you ever get the urge to say what you really feel? And oh, yes, I meant to tell you that I find you and Martin staying in separate rooms very quaint and old-fashioned. Is this for my benefit or is it standard procedure?"

"We aren't . . . we haven't . . ." she stopped.

"Saving yourself for marriage?" he inquired archly.

Helene didn't know what to say.

"You haven't actually convinced him that you're a virgin, have you?" Chris asked.

Helene's eyes filled with tears of frustration. The last thing on earth she wanted was a nasty scene with Martin's brother, but there was only so much a self-respecting person could take without striking back. Deciding that retreat was best, she turned to go and caught her heel on the edge of the wool rug in the center of the living room. The glass flew out of her hand and shattered against the wall. Crying openly now, aghast at her own clumsiness, Helene stumbled blindly and stepped on a shard, yelping in pain.

Chris was at her side in an instant, catching her and scooping her quickly into his arms.

"Take it easy, take it easy," he said softly. "The cut isn't bad, it doesn't look deep, there are some bandages in the kitchen. Just relax and let me carry you."

For several long, luxurious moments Helene did just that, dropping her head against his shoulder and closing her eyes. He felt so solid and strong and he smelled wonderful, a combination of the starch in his shirt, the soap he used and the clean, masculine scent of his skin. She sighed and relaxed, then realized what she was doing. Her eyes flew open in alarm. Martin's brother was holding her close, she was in his arms and she was enjoying it! She began to struggle, flailing out at him wildly.

"Put me down," she hissed, kicking her legs. "Let me go!"

"You can't stand on that foot," he said, holding on to her tightly while ducking her blows. "Will you stop that?"

"What the hell is going on here?" Martin said from the hall.

Two

Chris and Helene both looked up guiltily, as if caught in a criminal act.

"Helene cut her foot," Chris said.

"I cut my foot," Helene said miserably at the same time, blushing furiously.

"I see that," Martin replied, looking from one to the other and then down at the offended member, which was dripping scarlet onto the rug.

"Bring her into the kitchen," Martin commanded, and Chris obeyed, depositing Helene on a chair and then standing back, as if demonstrating that he had no claim on her.

"I'll take care of this," Martin said shortly.

Chris looked at Helene, who refused to meet his eyes. He hesitated for a moment and then abruptly left the room. They heard his bedroom door close smartly a few seconds later.

"So how did this happen?" Martin asked, removing a bottle of peroxide and a box of gauze from a cabinet. He got a plastic basin from the cubbyhole under the sink and a roll of tape from a drawer.

"I couldn't sleep and got up to get some milk," Helene replied. "On the way back I tripped on the living room rug and broke the glass."

"And how did Chris get involved?" Martin asked, pulling up his pajama legs as he knelt to slide the basin under her foot and then pour peroxide over the wound. Helene winced at the sting.

"He was up too, having a drink. He came to help." That was substantially the truth, but Helene still felt uncomfortably like a liar. Why? She wasn't really concealing anything—except her sudden, unexplained feelings.

"There," Martin said, drying the cut, which was bleeding less, and then covering it with gauze. He taped the dressing in place and stood up decisively, grunting with satisfaction.

"That should hold up pretty well," he said.

"Thank you," Helene said meekly, avoiding his gaze. "I'm sorry I woke you with my caterwauling."

"I couldn't imagine what was happening," Martin said, smiling slightly.

"Chris just picked me up and carried me off; I don't like to be manhandled that way," she said weakly, feeling that further clarification was necessary.

"That's my brother. He's a take-charge type of guy," Martin said, grinning.

His innocent acceptance of her explanation served to make Helene feel much worse and she wondered why. After all, nothing had happened, certainly nothing tangible enough to cause the surge of guilt she was experiencing.

"Do you want a pain pill?" Martin asked. "I have some left from a prescription for an abscessed tooth."

"No, it's not that bad. Suddenly I feel exhausted— I'm sure I'll be able to sleep now."

"Let me help you back to your room."

Helene leaned heavily on Martin's arm as they walked back to her door. He kissed her gently on the forehead and said, "Sleep well. I'll see you in the morning."

Helene nodded and closed the door, barely making it back to the bed before bursting into tears. She muffled her sobs with the bedspread, afraid of drawing Martin's attention again.

What on earth was wrong with her? She wasn't usually this emotional, in fact her customary stability was a point of pride. Through all of her recent troubles no one had seen her shed a tear. And now here she was bawling like a two-year-old because her fiancé's brother had held her for thirty seconds for a perfectly acceptable reason.

But that wasn't the problem and she knew it. The green memory of her reaction to the embrace was causing this cataract, and try as she might she could not put the sensation of Chris's arms around her out of her mind. She knew that if he'd tried to kiss her during those few fleeting moments he had held her, she would have responded.

Was it possible to be a loose woman and not know it? Maybe the potential had been there all the time, just waiting for the right button to be pushed. She didn't deserve Martin, that was clear, but she would try to make up for it. His brother's instinctive attempt to help her when she was hurt had produced a response in her she could never have anticipated and now must try feverishly to forget.

Helene sniffed loudly. Maybe that wouldn't be so difficult. After all, she would not have to see very much of Chris. She could make some excuse to cut this trip short, the wedding would be only one day and then she and Martin would be living back East. A Christmas visit once a year, maybe the occasional summer vacation stopover, that was all she would have to endure.

Heartened by these thoughts, Helene dried her eyes on a corner of the counterpane and settled back on the bed. She was not going to examine her reasons for making desperate plans to avoid Martin's brother for the rest of her life scant hours after meeting him. She punched the pillow and rolled over on her side, determined to get a couple of hours' sleep before the sun rose.

* * *

Chris gave up on sleep at five in the morning and took a shower. He dressed in the semidarkness, pulling on a clean pair of jeans and a T-shirt by the window, watching the streaks of orange and purple inflaming the sky. He clenched and unclenched his fists. His hands retained the feel of her, the slim body, the satiny skin, the brush of her silken hair against his wrist. Her fresh, flowery scent still seemed to surround him like a cloud; he saw again the outline of her body through the thin nightgown she wore as she stood before the fire. He sighed and closed his eyes. Martin's girl, of all people. What a mess. He had certainly not expected to feel like this about her.

To begin with, she wasn't at all what he had anticipated. He had been ready for some worldly, brassy number who knew the score, and instead here was this sweet, fragile, willowy type who blushed every time he looked at her. The innocence was all an act, of course, it had to be, but she was undoubtedly good at it. So good that he had forgotten it was a sham himself when he'd scooped her into his arms. He had wanted to carry her straight into his bedroom and he was afraid she knew it.

He turned away from the lightening sky with a sober expression, his mouth a grim line. He could handle it. He would keep his distance during their visit and then they would be gone. He was used to being denied what he wanted, and if his desire for this girl had taken him by surprise, it wasn't the first shock he'd endured. Not for the world would he disturb his brother's plans. After long years of living without affection or purpose, his faith in human nature had been restored by Martin. Of all the people he knew, Martin most deserved to be happy. He, Chris, would be distant and matter-of-fact with Helene when he saw her, which wouldn't be often; she would be living fifteen hundred miles away, after all. Martin would never have to know.

Comforted by this resolve, Chris went down to the kitchen to make coffee.

Chris had already finished eating and was out at the branding when Martin and Helene came down to breakfast. Maria de Salvo, the family housekeeper who had worked for Martin's father, poured juice into glasses as she said to them, "That boy hardly ate a thing, I wonder if he's coming down with something." She smiled at Helene. "I'm so glad to meet you, it's about time this one here settled down. Now if we could just find someone nice for Chris..."

"These eggs are delicious," Helene interjected quickly. "Did you put cheese in them?"

"My secret recipe," Maria said proudly.

"Nothing like it," Martin pronounced, through a mouthful. He glanced down at Helene's leg. "How's your foot?"

"Much better," Helene said.

"What happened?" Maria asked.

Helene gave her version of the incident and Maria said, "That Chris, he's a good man to have around in a crisis."

Helene let that pass.

They chatted through the meal and then Helene helped Maria clear the table. After the housekeeper had set the dishwasher churning she went off to do her other chores and Helene sat back at the table for a final cup of coffee with Martin.

"So, what shall we do today?" Martin asked. "Chris will be back at noon—would you like a tour of the ranch?"

"That would be lovely, of course, but..." Helene's voice trailed off into silence.

"What? What is it?"

"Martin, maybe we shouldn't stay as long as we planned," Helene said flatly.

"Why?"

"Come on, Martin, don't be obtuse. Chris doesn't like me."

"Oh, honey, you just don't understand him. I know he's difficult, but once you get to know him better you'll see that it's all a smokescreen, just talk. He distrusts strangers and right now you fall into that category. Give him a chance."

"He acts like I'm about to bind and gag you and ravish you behind a potted palm."

Martin grinned. "Doesn't sound like a bad idea."

"Martin, be serious. I don't think we should force a touchy situation that could become explosive. You wanted me to meet Chris, I've met him. Let's spend the rest of the day here and then go back East. I don't want to come between you and your brother and I'm afraid that may happen if we stay."

Martin said nothing, but she could see that he was considering it, albeit reluctantly.

"Isn't it better to let him get used to the idea of our getting married gradually? Why press this now, when he's obviously having a hard time with it?"

Martin sat back in his chair, sighing. "All right. But I promise you if you give him a break you'll be rewarded. He's wary and take my word for it, that's perfectly understandable. If you'd had his experiences you would be too."

"I don't doubt it," Helene said, feeling her tension ease palpably. He was going to listen to her.

"What can I tell him about why we're leaving so soon?"

"A white lie. I was planning to mail in the computer sheets for my final grade reports, but we can say I discovered an error and have to go back to correct it personally."

"I see you've already thought this out," Martin observed.

"I had plenty of time to think last night when I couldn't sleep," she replied.

"All right," Martin said, standing. "Let's go find him."

Chris accepted the news of their imminent departure with such poorly concealed relief that Helene was glad she had suggested it. They went through with the formality of the ranch tour and somehow Helene was able to make the appropriate responses when Chris pointed out this or that improvement as they racketed around the dirt paths between the animal pens in his jeep. She admired the stainless-steel feeding trough and the mechanized drinking fountain, the cedar corral fence and the new turf in the lower paddock. She had never been on a livestock ranch before and had no idea what any of it was, but the thought that she would be escaping Chris's disturbing presence very shortly sustained her. By the time they got back it was necessary to pack and head out to the airport. She wasn't alone with Chris again until Martin took their baggage out to the car and she was left with his brother in the living room.

"So," Chris said evenly.

Helene looked at him.

"I guess I've driven you away."

"Not at all. Martin told you why I have to go back..."

Chris waved his hand in dismissal, cutting off her explanation. "Please give me a little credit," he said evenly. "I may not be a brain trust like my older brother, but even I know when I'm being subjected to a snow job."

Helene met his eyes, then looked away, feeling naked under his penetrating gaze.

"I'm just not as easy to fool as he is, am I?" he said quietly, insinuatingly, and then he turned away as Martin bustled back into the room.

They said their goodbyes at the house, as Martin was going to drive back to the airport and leave the rental car there. Helene avoided Chris's glance as he clasped her hand in farewell and she didn't look at him again until she was safely in the car and he was standing at the front door watching them leave. Why did she feel such an overwhelming sense of flight from doom, as if she had narrowly avoided a disaster?

As was usually the case with travel, the journey back seemed shorter than the trip out and as they circled Newark airport preparing for landing Helene relaxed for the first time since she had met Chris Murdock.

She was far away from him. Everything would certainly be all right now.

Everything was not all right. The memory of Chris's embrace haunted her. Why didn't she feel that same sinking, languorous sensation when Martin touched her? Something was wrong. If she had suspected it before she met Chris, she knew it now. It wasn't long before Helene had convinced herself that what was lacking was a physical relationship with her fiancé. Surely if she made love with Martin, all her doubts would be swept aside. They were to be married shortly anyway, what difference would it make if they got a head start on the honeymoon? She would forget those stolen seconds in Chris's arms in his brother's bed.

They had only been back from Wyoming for a few days when Helene cooked a special dinner for Martin in his apartment. While they were relaxing afterward she said, "I've been thinking."

"Oh, oh," Martin replied, looking at her over his newspaper.

"Maybe I should stay the night," she said, smiling.

Martin set the paper aside carefully. "Does that mean what I think it means?"

"It does."

He rose and came to her side, sitting on the arm of her chair. "What brought this on? As I recall, you were the one who wanted to wait. You said it would make the marriage ceremony more special if . . ."

"I know what I said," Helene replied, interrupting him as she suppressed a surge of irritation. "I thought it was a woman's prerogative to change her mind. After all, we're both adults and it seems silly of me to cling to such a quaint, old-fashioned notion." She stopped. Was she quoting Chris Murdock?

Martin leaned over to kiss her warmly. "I thought it was a charming notion, but of course if you really have changed your mind . . ." He started to laugh.

"I have," she said.

He got up and extended his hand. Helene rose and took it and Martin led the way to his bedroom.

Ninety minutes later Martin was asleep and Helene was sitting in the living room, staring unseeingly at a television sitcom and nursing a cup of tea. Martin's flannel robe was wrapped around her and the scent of him imbedded in the cloth brought to mind her sexual initiation, which had just taken place.

Well, she had gotten what she wanted. And Martin had been wonderful, really. Sweet, tender, understanding. No virgin could have had a more compassionate lover. So then why did she feel like crying?

Helene bit her lip resolutely. No more tears. She was not going to turn into a quivering wreck over an immature infatuation with her husband's brother, a man who clearly couldn't stand her. So what if her first experience with Martin had not driven him from her mind? Everyone said these things took time. Women who expected fireworks during defloration were always disappointed.

Helene took a sip of her drink, tracing the healing cut on her bare foot with her finger. She had to silence the nagging whisper that said the problem was not her lack of experience but her choice of men. The truth was she had been more excited by a few seconds of closeness with Chris than an hour in bed with Martin. And, of course, it was possible that she was just a spoiled child who only wanted what she knew she couldn't have. She sighed. Neither prospect presented her with an appealing picture of herself.

Helene stood up briskly and walked into Martin's kitchen, dumping the rest of her drink down the drain.

Time would pass, she would make a life with Martin, she would forget his brother.

That's all there was to it.

Six weeks later Helene was painting a wall in Martin's apartment, readying the place for her upcoming wedding, when the telephone rang. She climbed down off the ladder and set the roller in the tray on the floor, paused on her way past the air-conditioning control to lower the temperature, then lifted the receiver.

"Hello?" she said.

"Helene?" a man responded.

Helene froze. She had only met him once, but she knew his voice. It was Martin's brother.

"Helene, are you there? This is Chris."

Helene leaned against the wall and closed her eyes. "Yes?" she replied weakly.

"Helene, I have bad news," he said flatly.

She straightened, alert. "What is it?"

"Martin is dead."

Helene stared blankly at Martin's white refrigerator. "What?" she whispered.

"I said Martin is dead. He was killed in a car accident early this morning."

"What are you talking about—? He's on a business trip to Atlanta. I just spoke to him last night."

"He was on his way to that law firm down there for a breakfast meeting when his car collided with a truck. Everybody in the car was killed." He paused. "I'm sorry," he added curtly.

The room seemed to be spinning around her. She sat down hard at the kitchen table.

"Are you there?" Chris said.

Helene cleared her throat. "Yes." She thought a moment. "Are you calling from Wyoming?"

"Yes. I just heard from the hospital about ten minutes ago," he replied.

"Why did they call you instead of me?"

"He had a next-of-kin card in his wallet, an old one he'd filled out years ago, and it named me. Maybe he meant to change it when he got married, I don't know," Chris answered.

"It doesn't matter." Her thoughts were tumbling over themselves. "What should we do?"

"That's what I wanted to ask you. Should I have the body flown up to New Jersey? Do you want to have the funeral there?"

The body. He was talking about Martin. Oh, God. She was silent for so long that Chris thought she had hung up.

"I think he would want to be buried on the ranch," Helene said softly. "Go back to his roots, you know?"

"I thought that too, but his colleagues are there by you, the people he worked with for years. He lived in the East for a long time."

"We'll send out notices to the people here, maybe have a chapel service, whatever you think best. But he would want to be buried with his father."

There was a long pause, and then Chris said, "I agree." Was there a catch in his voice?

"What do you want me to do?" Helene asked.

"I'll call Atlanta and make the arrangements to bring Martin home," Chris said. "When can you get here?"

"I'll catch the first available plane."

"Let me know," Chris said shortly and hung up with a resounding click.

Helene slumped in her chair. Maybe she was having a nightmare. Maybe Martin wasn't dead. If she could just wake up...

Pull yourself together, she told herself sternly. You have to think of Martin, to do everything the way he would have wanted it done.

She picked up the phone again to book a flight.

* * *

The funeral took place on a burning August day. It seemed forever before the people who gathered at the house afterward dispersed and went their various ways. Helene helped Maria put away the leftover food and bag the trash. Then at dusk Maria went back to her family in town and Helene wandered into the living room to find Chris sitting in the same chair he had occupied the night she broke the glass. How long ago that seemed. She dropped onto the loveseat opposite him and they sat in silence for a while before Chris said, "Well, I guess it's all over for you now, isn't it?"

"What do you mean?"

"The gravy train has left without you. Too bad Martin didn't die after the wedding—you would have come into quite a bit."

Helene stood up and began to walk out.

"Oh, leave, that's right," Chris called after her. "You don't have to put up with me now, there's nothing to be gained by it."

Helene turned on her heel and marched resolutely over to him. "Do you have to make this day more difficult than it's already been?" she demanded.

"Why not? Why not get it all out in the open now? We've been tiptoeing around one another long enough."

"I don't have to listen to this. My connection with you is over. Your brother is dead and after today I never plan to see you again."

"Not even to collect the money for your family's trust?" Chris said meanly, standing to face her.

Helene stared at him.

"He wrote it to survive him, didn't you know? Your mother and sister get a monthly stipend. That doesn't change, but guess what? Nothing for you. You were supposed to marry him, of course, but now that seems to be off, so what next? Beating the bushes for bachelor number two? You'd better step lively, that skinny savings account of yours won't hold out for long."

Helene stared at him, her mouth agape. "What do you know about my savings account?"

He folded his arms and regarded her levelly. "I had you investigated after you were out here last time."

Helene was shocked into silence. She couldn't believe it.

"I had every right to protect my brother. He was too trusting for his own good," Chris said defensively.

"And what did you find, mastermind?" Helene countered. "That I was an agent of a foreign power, that I was drugging Martin to get him under my spell, that he had signed over all his wordly goods to me? You found exactly nothing, that's what, or you would have told Martin all about it back then."

Chris made no reply.

"As I'm sure you discovered from your expensive private investigation, my interest in your brother was not financial. I do have a job, you know, and I will keep it. I was marrying your brother because he was a fine man who..."

"I know he was a fine man. I also know you didn't love him," Chris said expressionlessly.

"How dare you say that?"

"Because it's true. You were very nice to him. I dare say you liked him and you undoubtedly liked his money a lot more, but you didn't love him. He was a way out of your troubles, that's all."

"I would have made him a wonderful wife!"

"Oh, I'm sure you would have been dutiful. Especially in bed. I mean, you would have seen it as your duty to please him, but you would have been as enthusiastic about it as a whore servicing her most important customer."

Helene slapped him as hard as she could.

"Truth hurts, huh?" he said, raising his hand to touch his cheek, which turned white, then scarlet.

They stared at one another, the atmosphere so charged it could have presaged an electrical storm. Why did he always have to look so good, Helene wondered miserably? Even now, when she wanted to kill him, she wanted to caress him still more, and the knowledge of her own weakness fueled her anger.

"From the moment you met me you've done nothing but bait me and treat me abominably," she whispered finally. "Why?"

"I don't like phonies."

"Why are you so certain I am one?"

"Women who pretend to be in love in order to solve their financial problems are phonies."

"You just keep repeating the same insults—do you have to convince yourself of this garbage in order to justify your treatment of me? You're disgusting."

"I'm disgusting? You were planning to marry a man for whom you felt not an iota of desire or passion and *I'm* disgusting?"

"You can't know what I felt," Helene said, turning away from him.

"I know what you didn't feel," he said. "I've seen women physically in love and, believe me, you weren't one of them."

"Oh, I'm sure you're a great expert on the physical side of love," Helene said sarcastically.

"Do you doubt it?" he said, staring her down, and she could feel the heat creeping up her neck.

"There are other things in the world besides sex, things two people can share in a marriage," Helene replied. "There's mutual respect and caring and a reverence for the same way of life and . . ."

"All of that was going to keep your bed warm?" Chris interjected. "Poor Martin. Maybe he's better off dead."

Helene gasped. "You bastard," she cried, pushing past him and running down the hall to her room. She locked the door behind her and, trembling, began flinging items into the single bag she'd brought.

She would be all right when she got home, to her family and the job that was due to resume in September. Over the summer she would have plenty of time to think about the baby.

She sat down on the edge of the bed. On the way out to Wyoming she had stopped at a pharmacy and purchased a home pregnancy test, and before the funeral that morning she had taken it.

The results were positive.

The fluid in the test tube turning pink had only confirmed what she already knew; she had always been regular and she was now a month overdue. She and Martin had taken no precautions because they thought they'd be married soon. Helene had half hoped for a baby to give her something positive to concentrate on, Martin's child to drive the specter of Chris Murdock from her thoughts.

Now that Martin was dead, of course, she would have to carry on alone with the baby. It would be difficult, money would be tight and she would have to find suitable day care, but if she had been able to endure the time since Martin's death, she was convinced that she could now stand anything.

She remembered the box from the pregnancy test, which she had carefully wrapped in its brown paper bag and stowed at the bottom of the wastepaper basket. On second thought, she decided to put it back into her overnight case and take it with her.

She went over to the basket and discovered that it had been emptied. Maria, of course. Helene should have thought of that, but she was not used to servants following after her and tidying up her room. Oh well, it was just a brown bag—it might have contained somebody's discarded lunch. Maria had probably put it outside already. But just to be on the safe side Helene decided to go down to the kitchen and see if Maria had left it in the plastic container there prior to taking it out to the shed. Now I'm reduced to picking through garbage, Helene thought, sneaking past the empty living room. She was bending over the receptacle and rummaging through its contents when Chris said behind her, "Looking for this?"

Helene whirled to face him. He was holding the empty blue box by its flap, swinging it back and forth.

Helene felt her blood begin to thunder in her ears. "Where did you get that?" she demanded.

He smiled unpleasantly. "No defense like a good offense, huh?" he said.

"Have you been going through my things?" she asked angrily, her mind racing wildly.

"Didn't have to. Maria found this in your room and thought I should see it."

"I didn't realize that Maria was your spy."

"Maria is very loyal to this family and did absolutely the right thing. I haven't heard an explanation yet."

"And you won't. What I do with my life from now on is none of your business."

"It is my business if you're carrying my brother's kid!"

Helene said nothing.

"I'm not even going to ask why a syrupy little self-declared virgin like Helene Sweetness Danforth would have use for one of these."

"I don't have to answer your questions."

"At least, I assume it's yours," he went on, as if she hadn't spoken. "I know it's not mine and Maria says it's not hers, and I believe her since she's sixty-two."

"Maybe one of your girlfriends left it there," Helene responded.

"Don't get cute with me," he said angrily. "I thought you told me that you weren't sleeping with Martin until after the wedding!"

Helene stared at him. Is that what was bothering him, that she had slept with his brother?

"I suppose I should be grateful that you're assuming the baby is Martin's," she said.

"Then there is a baby."

She sighed; he would find out anyway. "Yes."

"And it is Martin's?"

She looked away from him. "Don't be ridiculous. Of course it's Martin's."

He threw the box across the room, narrowly missing her head. "What happened to the purity-until-marriage kick?" he said furiously.

"I . . . changed my mind," she said shortly.

"So it was your idea?" he asked.

"What difference does it make?" she said wearily.

"Why did you change your mind?"

Helene wasn't going to touch that topic. "What are you, the FBI? I suppose now you'll want to run blood tests or something, to prove paternity."

"I don't know how tests can be performed on a corpse six feet under the ground."

Helene winced at this description of his brother, her eyes filling with tears.

He tilted his head back in a characteristic gesture and eyed her narrowly. "What are you going to do?"

"I'm going to have it, if that's what you're asking," turning her head to wipe her eyes discreetly.

"And raise an illegitimate child?"

"I have little choice about it."

He shook his head. "Oh, no. I won't have Martin's kid go through what I did: the snide remarks, the snickering, the empty seat on Father's Day at school."

"And what is your solution?" Helene asked sarcastically.

"I think we should get married."

Three

Several endless seconds of deafening silence went by before Helene burst into peals of helpless laughter; there was more than a tinge of hysteria in it.

"You think I'm being funny?" Chris said tightly.

"Wait a minute," she said, waving her hand helplessly, when she could talk. "Let me get this straight. You detest me, you've made that very clear. You think I'm a money-grubbing gold digger who came close to duping your brother, but now that you have the chance to be rid of me, instead of packing me off forever with a profound sense of relief, you are asking me to *marry* you?"

"For the baby's sake," he said tonelessly.

"Well, I didn't think it was for mine," she replied, coughing and wiping her eyes.

He looked back at her, unperturbed. "I'm serious," he said.

Helene met his frank gaze.

Apparently he was.

"You weren't even going to tell me about the baby, were you?" he said softly.

"Why should I? I didn't expect you to greet the news with shouts of joy. I am its mother, after all, and we already know what you think of me, don't we?"

"Martin was its father and I'm its uncle."

"Oh, then I take it there is some good blood involved?" she said sarcastically.

"I want to take responsibility for the child," he said, ignoring her tone.

"You can't force me to marry you," she shot back.

"Think of the baby, Helene," he said. It was the first time she could remember him using her name.

"I am thinking of the baby."

"You're thinking of yourself. You don't like me..?"

She glared at him stonily.

"All right, maybe it's more than dislike. Since you feel that way you want to run back to New Jersey and have the child alone, to prove to the world and to me that you don't need anybody. But have you thought of what that will mean for the kid?"

"I will take care of it . . ." she began fiercely.

"You don't know what you're talking about," he interrupted her, shaking his head disgustedly. "People may say that in today's world illegitimacy doesn't matter, but I know from firsthand experience that it does," he said quietly. "It will come to haunt your child in many ways that you can't even imagine right now."

Helene said nothing. She couldn't argue with him there, he was the expert on that subject.

"All you can think of at this moment is getting away from me and with the baby safe inside you anything seems possible," Chris continued. "But in a few months it will have a life of its own and the decision you make today will affect that life from day one and forever. I'm offering you a way out of bearing a fatherless child, the blank space on the birth certificate, the whole shot. Think about it."

Helene looked away from him pensively.

"The trust will provide for your family, you don't have to worry about them. And we'll stay married just until the baby is born." He cleared his throat. "I promise I won't touch you while we're together and I'll release you with alimony and child support when it's over and we go our separate ways.

"Why, Chris?" she whispered finally. "Why would you do all that for me?"

"I would be doing it for Martin, who was the best person I ever knew," he said simply. "Ninety-nine out of a hundred guys would have resented the hell out of me when I appeared on the scene, Johnny-come-lately, moving in on his home territory, instant family. Martin was that one in one hundred, and I'll never forget him. I want to do my best for his kid. Is that so difficult to understand?"

Helene sighed, then shook her head.

"So what do you say?" he prodded.

"I have my job," she said feebly. "I will need it for . . . afterward, after the divorce."

"Can't you get a leave of absence?"

"I don't know. The board of education would have to approve it. I could try." She eyed him warily. "You would want me to live here on the ranch, I assume."

He nodded. "For as long as it takes, until the baby is born. When is it due?"

"March 20."

"It's now the beginning of August. You arrange your leave and come back here and we can be married by the end of the month."

Helene tried to imagine living with him and couldn't. The two of them alone in this house?

"Separate bedrooms," Chris added quickly, as if reading her mind. "I go my own way, no questions asked, and you're free to do exactly the same. Deal?"

Helene hesitated. "What about Maria? She'll know, I mean, she'll see the bedrooms."

"You let me handle Maria," he said shortly.

"Don't fire her," Helene said quickly, not wanting to be responsible for it.

Chris smiled slightly. "You're worried about Maria's job? Have you forgotten who ratted on you today?"

"I can understand loyalty," Helene answered shortly. "It's a concept I've embraced myself, once or twice."

"You're stalling. Do we have a deal?" he said.

She closed her eyes. "Yes."

"Good," he said lightly. "Now go back to New Jersey and get that leave of absence."

The superintendent of schools was a friend of Martin's, and Helene's leave was approved by the board of education without debate. By the end of August she was back in Wyoming and about to marry Christopher Murdock.

She hadn't even told her family what she was doing. Her sister Peggy was too young to know what was going on and her mother accepted the story of teaching in the West for a year on an exchange program without question. After she had the baby Helene would deal with the rest of it.

One thing at a time.

On the day of her wedding Helene patted her hair into place and adjusted the belt on her dress, then glanced at the closet where her clothes had recently been hung. Chris had put her into the guest bedroom she'd occupied when visiting with Martin, then told her to be ready at two o'clock for the trip to the registry office. They'd gotten the license and taken the blood tests; there was nothing left to do except get married. Helene thought for a moment of the wedding she'd anticipated with the other Murdock brother, then dismissed it wearily from her mind. Nobody but Maria and Sam, the ranch hand, knew that she had been engaged to Martin. Her visit in June had been so brief that they'd had no time for socializing.

She was grateful for that now, it would spare her a lot of explanations.

When she emerged from her room Chris was waiting for her. He was dressed soberly in a light gray suit that contrasted handsomely with his dark hair and eyes, and he was holding a square florist's box gingerly in his left hand. He extended it to her wordlessly.

Helene accepted it in surprise, opening the glassine cover of the container and taking out a waxy camellia.

"I . . . I wasn't expecting anything," she said honestly, stroking a dewy petal of the flower with her finger.

"I know it isn't much," he said, clearly uncomfortable. "I just thought you should have . . . something."

"Thank you," Helene said quietly, slipping the band over her wrist and picking up her purse.

They drove into town in the sports car with the top down, Helene watching the lush summer scenery pass in silence. Another couple was ahead of them at the registry and their obvious happiness contrasted bleakly with the gloom enfolding Chris and Helene. When their turn came, the jovial justice insisted on Chris "kissing the bride," which resulted in a dry peck on the cheek for Helene. The justice remarked, grinning, that he hoped Chris would be able to do better than that on the honeymoon and it seemed an eternity before the short civil service was finally over and they could leave.

Maria de Salvo and her husband, who had served as witnesses, were waiting by the door.

"Mrs. Murdock," Maria said, as Chris took her husband aside to talk to him. Helene turned at the name; she had expected to be Mrs. Murdock, just not *this* Mrs. Murdock.

"Yes, Maria?" she said.

"I wanted to talk to you..." Maria twisted her hands nervously. "I told Mr. Chris about the pregnancy test I found in the trash."

Helene nodded. "I know."

"I suppose you're angry with me," she said anxiously.

Helene sighed. "It's all water under the bridge, Maria. I understand why you did it and it's over now. Why don't we just forget it?"

A relieved smile spread over the housekeeper's face. "I'm glad you feel that way."

"I do."

"Then I'll be in tomorrow morning as usual?" Maria said.

"Of course. I don't want to disturb your schedule." I won't be around that long anyway, Helene added silently.

Maria's husband came to join her and after exchanging a few more pleasantries with Helene the de Salvos left.

"Not exactly the wedding of your dreams, was it?" Chris said behind her.

Helene turned to look up into his dark eyes. "I didn't have any illusions about it," she said simply.

"I gave Maria the rest of the day off, so I guess we'd better get some dinner before we head back to the ranch," he said.

"I can make something, if you'd prefer," Helene replied.

"You're going to cook for me?" he said, surprised.

"Why not? I'm far from helpless, you know."

He measured her with his unsettling gaze. "I wasn't expecting it," he said in his blunt, unvarnished way.

"Does such domesticity make it seem too much like a real marriage?" Helene asked guilelessly.

He didn't answer, his lips thinning into a grim line.

"Chris, we don't necessarily have to be enemies, do we?" Helene asked him softly.

"Let's go," he said shortly, not answering her. "I have some work I want to finish up tonight."

By the time they got back to the Homestead it was after five and the ranch hands were drifting in toward the bunkhouses, working the outside pumps to clean up for the evening meal.

"Are you sure you want to do this?" Chris asked, as Helene investigated the kitchen to see what was on hand. "I can just go out back and eat with the hands."

"On your wedding night?" Helene said dryly. "Not a chance." She took out some defrosted chicken parts and poured safflower oil in a pan to heat for frying.

Chris sat at the kitchen table, draping his suit jacket across the back of his chair and pulling his tie loose from its knot. He watched in silence as she went about the dinner preparations, his eyes burning a hole in her back.

"Is the branding going well?" she asked, removing the ingredients she needed from cabinets and the refrigerator as she found them.

"Well as can be expected."

"I thought branding was done in the spring."

"These are late summer calves," he replied briefly, without further explanation.

"So how is the ranch doing in general?" Helene asked brightly in desperation, thinking that if he didn't stop staring at her she would begin to scream.

"Fine," he said.

"Is it profitable?" she asked, dipping each piece of chicken in beaten egg and then rolling it in bread crumbs.

"Very," he said shortly. "Don't worry, I'll have no trouble coming up with the child support."

Helene turned to face him, keeping her temper under control with an effort. "I've already told you I don't want any money. That's not why I asked."

"Well?" he said challengingly, shrugging.

"Just trying to make conversation," she said, turning back to the stove.

"Why?" he countered maddeningly.

"I can't imagine," she muttered, tossing the chicken into the oil with such force that it sputtered. She worked on in silence, feeling like a laboratory mouse being inspected by a clinician. She finally set a plate before him without comment and then sat across from him, picking up her fork and toying with her own food. The ticking of the kitchen clock sounded loud in the silence.

"Cat got your tongue?" Chris said inquiringly around a mouthful of chicken.

"You seem to find everything I say annoying. I'm trying not to irritate you."

"Is that what it is? I find it irritating."

Helene dropped her fork with a clatter and brushed past him. He seized her arm and stood, kicking his chair out of the way.

"Let me go," she said fiercely.

"You haven't finished eating."

"I'm not hungry," she almost yelled, close to tears.

"You should eat, you know, for the baby. I guess I should have told you . . . it's very good."

Helene stared up at him, stunned. After torturing her for the past couple of hours, he was now going to compliment her on her cooking? What was going on in his mind?

At this happy juncture the doorbell rang.

"Who the hell is that?" Chris muttered, releasing Helene and leaving the kitchen to answer it. Helene trailed after him curiously.

He opened the door to admit a stunning blonde who flung herself into his arms.

"Christy," she exclaimed, "where the hell have you been? Nobody down at Brodie's has seen you for the last couple of weeks and we were beginning to wonder if you'd taken the pledge." She kissed him lingeringly on the mouth and then drew back to examine Helene.

"My brother died," Chris said shortly.

The girl's expression changed. "I didn't even know you had a brother," she said.

"He had been living back East for years. I brought him out here to bury him."

"Gee, I'm sorry," she said, nonplussed. Then she nodded at Helene. "Who's this?"

"My wife," Chris said.

The girl's mouth fell open unglamorously.

"Your what?" she said.

"Wife," Chris repeated, enunciating clearly. "Ginny Porter, meet Helene Murdock."

Ginny disengaged herself from Chris and smiled weakly at Helene. "How do you do?" she said nervously, tucking her billowing hair behind her ear.

"Hello," Helene said.

"So, how long have you been married?" Ginny asked.

Chris looked at his watch.

"Three and a half hours," he said.

"Kind of sudden, wasn't it?" Ginny said, looking from one to the other in amazement.

"You could say that," Helene replied dryly.

"Look, Ginny, we're just in the middle of dinner," Chris said, taking her by the hand and leading her toward the door. "Tell Brodie I'll be in soon to see him."

"That's why I'm here," Ginny said, turning to face him. "If you want to participate in the rodeo you have to register by Friday, and we were all wondering if you forgot about it."

"What rodeo?" Helene asked.

"Just a small amateur thing sponsored by the chamber of commerce," Chris said dismissively.

"It is not," Ginny protested. "It's an all-county event and Chris has been calf-roping champion the last three years running. You don't mean to say he never told you about that?"

"Never said a word," Helene replied wonderingly.

Chris opened the front door and practically levitated Ginny through it. "Thanks for the reminder. I'll be in to register," he said hastily, pushing her forward with his hand splayed against the small of her back. "See you soon. Bye." He slammed the door closed behind her.

"So who was that, Christy?" Helene asked mildly.

"Barmaid down at Brodie's, the local watering hole," he replied, not meeting her eyes.

"Fan of yours?"

"We went out a few times."

"Did you see the look on her face when you told her I was your wife? She couldn't have been more surprised if you'd told her I was your grandmother."

He grunted.

"Do you think we'll be visited by any more of your little friends? Maybe we should send out a newsletter to spread the glad tidings of your marriage to all of Brodie's customers."

He threw her a dirty look and headed back to the kitchen, dragging her behind him by her wrist.

"Sit," he said, pointing to her chair. "I want to see you eat something. You're supposed to be gaining weight, not losing it, and you look thinner than when you were out here in June."

Helene picked up a lukewarm chicken leg obediently and nibbled it gingerly.

"I guess a lot of people will be as shocked as Ginny was to hear we're married," she observed.

"Don't worry about them."

"How about Sam?"

"I told him what he needs to know."

Helene could only imagine what that meant. She sat staring into space with the chicken leg in her hand.

He looked up from his plate and narrowed his eyes at her, pointing to her plate.

"I'm eating," she said, brandishing the drumstick and then taking a big bite of it.

Under his watchful eye she ate industriously until she was so full she felt she would not be able to get up from the table. When it came time to clear the dishes she stood up and then swayed unsteadily, grabbing for the back of her chair.

"What is it?" Chris said, at her side instantly.

"Little dizzy," she said fuzzily.

Chris bent to slip an arm under her legs and lifted her into his embrace.

"Bed for you," he said, moving toward the hall. "And I'm calling the doctor."

"No doctor. Pregnant women get dizzy, don't you know that? It's hormones or something," Helene said wearily, letting her head fall back against his shoulder.

"We'll see," he said grimly.

"You made me eat too much food," she protested weakly. "That's all it is, I feel sick."

He kicked open the door of her bedroom.

"You're always carrying me," she said dreamily. The well-remembered smell of him engulfed her and she turned her head to touch her nose to the warm skin exposed by the open collar of his shirt.

He sat on the edge of her bed and then eased her into position against the pillows. She looked up at him. The room *was* spinning and his face seemed to be fading in and out of her visual field. He started to move away and she clutched his arm.

"Stay with me," she whispered, succumbing to a sudden irrational fear of being alone. No matter how negative his opinion of her was, the one quality he exuded was strength and she needed that now.

"I'm not going anywhere," he said soothingly, "I was just reaching for the phone."

How nice he is when I'm in trouble, she thought dreamily. I should be in trouble all the time, cut my foot or pitch a faint, then he will always talk with this gentle note in his voice, instead of that hard, cynical tone I hate.

She heard him talking on the phone, the sound coming as if from a great distance, and then she was asleep.

Helene awoke several hours later to find Chris sitting next to her bed in a kitchen chair. She had a dim memory of the doctor's visit, his stern warnings about low blood pressure and exhaustion, but it all blended in with her dreams.

"What's the verdict?" she said, yawning.

"Dr. Stern says you're to stay in bed for the next several days, and if I have to handcuff you to the headboard you will do just that," he said grimly.

"Don't worry," Helene said quietly. "I know how much your brother's child means to you. I'll be good."

"I'm going to see that you are," he said. He stood and opened the door to admit Maria, who came in still wearing the dress she had worn to the wedding that afternoon.

"Oh, Chris, you didn't," Helene said in dismay. "This isn't fair to Maria, she has her own family."

"My children are grown and out of the house and my husband can do without me for a few days," Maria said briskly.

"So you're to be my watchdog?" Helene asked.

"We have to take special care of you," Maria replied, shooing Chris out of the room. When the door had closed behind him she added in a low tone, "That boy practically promised me the moon if I came here tonight. I think he's really worried."

"He loved Martin, the baby is important to him."

"But not you?" Maria asked softly.

"I'm the incubator," Helene said lightly.

Maria opened her mouth to speak, then thought better of it and settled for tucking the covers in around Helene's feet.

"Now," she said, "how about a nice cup of herbal tea?"

* * *

Once Maria was on the job, Chris virtually vanished. He was gone before Helene got up in the morning and he came in for dinner at night, bone weary, and ate anything Maria put in front of him. Then he went to his room, took a shower and changed and left again, doubtless for Brodie's or a similar destination. Sometimes Helene heard him come in before she fell asleep, but usually not. She had no idea how he could keep such hours and work so hard, and she had no idea what Maria thought of their somewhat peculiar living arrangements. Nothing was discussed.

When Dr. Stern returned in a week and pronounced Helene fit and rested, Maria went back home and Helene was allowed out of bed for the first time since the doctor's previous visit. For two more weeks she wandered around the house, bored by inactivity, while Chris stuck to his previous schedule: work during the day and disappearances after dinner. One night at the end of September, looking for something to do, Helene wandered down to the living room to find a book on the shelves by the fireplace and then settled down to read. She read until well past midnight and then finally fell asleep with the book in her lap, waking by the grandfather clock when Chris came in at two-thirty. He strode into the living room, spotted her on the couch and said wearily, " I thought you would be in bed."

He was wearing faded jeans that clung to him like a second skin, with woven moccasins and a yellow oxford-cloth shirt showing vividly against his suntanned throat. His sleeves were rolled up to his elbows, revealing the well-developed veins and tendons in his work-hardened forearms. His hair was tousled, doubtless from the homeward ride in his convertible. Helene wished, not for the first time, that she had the nerve, or the right, to stroke it back into place.

"I fell asleep reading," she answered, holding up the book.

"Poetry?" he said archly.

"Yours," she replied, thumbing to the flyleaf and displaying his name written there.

"I must have done that during one of my possessive periods," he said. "Martin was always taking my stuff." He folded his arms combatively. "Are you surprised that I read poetry? Or are you surprised that I can read?"

"Not at all, to both questions," she said lightly, putting the book aside.

He slumped next to her on the couch. "I've been drinking," he said almost belligerently, and smiled.

That was obvious, but he was not drunk—just clearly relaxed enough to lose his inhibitions. Warning bells went off in Helene's brain; without his customary control he would be dangerous indeed. She rose smoothly and stepped into her discarded slippers.

"Good night," she said.

"Wait a minute, where are you going?" he asked, waving her back into her seat. "Don't you want to know why I've been going out every night? Aren't you the least bit curious?"

"I have assumed the obvious, that you want to avoid me," she said evenly.

"Bingo," he responded. "Correctomundo, right the first time. But do you know *why* I want to avoid you?"

"Chris, is it really necessary to do this?" she asked, pained and a little frightened. Where was this leading?

"Certainly, certainly. Know the truth and the truth shall make you free. Don't you remember that one?"

Helene waited.

"I have wanted to avoid you because I have a secret, a secret very difficult to keep in your presence." He got up and helped himself to the bottle of Scotch on the sideboard, splashing a liberal dose of the amber liquid into a glass.

"Chris, don't drink any more," Helene said quietly.

"Oh, but I must. How else do I keep my secret, especially with you sitting there in that most fetching outfit?"

Helene glanced down at her cotton nightgown, as plain and practical as a nun's. What did he mean? She glanced up at him again, her expression guarded.

He wagged his finger at her. "You're humoring me, I can tell by that look of sainted patience on your face. Have I ever told you how much I hate that look?"

"You wouldn't have to see it if you'd let me go to bed," she pointed out reasonably.

"Bed," he said. "Now there's a subject of interest, actually in line with my first topic, one and the same, in fact."

Helene sighed. Booze certainly made him loquacious. Which was worse, his sober silences or this?

"Haven't guessed my secret?" he said, sipping. "Not a clue? Then I'll tell you. It's mundane, not original, very old I'm afraid. Biblical. Now what do you think of that?"

Helene was frozen in place.

"Don't know what I'm talking about, Miss Innocence?" he said, examining her with those unsettling eyes, the same color as the liquor he held in his hand.

But she did know what he was talking about. After three weeks of listening for his footfall, straining to catch the sound of his voice, fingering one of his discarded shirts cast over a chair, she knew all too well.

"I know," she whispered.

His sneer vanished and he thrust his glass onto the top of the television set. He was beside her in two strides and had seized her bare upper arms, holding her in a viselike grip.

"Please, Chris, you're hurting me," she gasped, twisting futilely in his grasp.

"I don't want to hurt you," he said gruffly, and then his mouth was on hers—hot, searching, the way she had dreamed of it since the first day she'd met him. For several seconds she was stunned, and then her arms crept up around his neck, her fingers sinking into the wealth of hair at his nape and her body molding itself to his.

When he saw that she was not fighting him and he felt her response, he moaned against her mouth and the sound turned her limbs to water. She clutched him as she kissed him back, her very lack of expertise inflaming his desire as he lifted her into his arms and onto the couch. They lay entwined as his lips trailed down her neck and inside the collar of her gown. She was wearing nothing beneath it; he fumbled with the buttons on the front to open it fully, then she whimpered as his mouth found her breast. Her eyes squeezed shut as his free hand trailed up her leg and to the inside of her thigh and then she surged up eagerly when he moved to kiss her again. Thought fled, time stood still as his tongue found hers and Helene submitted completely to his kisses. Too soon, he drew back slightly, still holding her fast.

"Do you want me?" he whispered harshly against her lips, pulling her lower body against his. She arched to meet him.

"Do you?" he prompted.

"Yes, yes," she moaned, drawing his head down to hers again, incapable of anything but desperate, headlong yearning.

"Then say it," he prompted.

"I want you," she sighed.

"Is that what you said to my brother?" he asked.

Four

―――

Helene shoved him off her with as much force as she could muster and then jumped to her feet, sputtering.

"You . . . you," she said and stopped, at a loss and shaking so hard she had to put a hand out to the wall for balance. She stared at him in malevolent silence; she just couldn't think of anything vile enough to call him.

"Bastard?" he supplied, sitting up and then vaulting easily to his feet. "Isn't that the word you're searching for—doubly appropriate in my case, don't you think?"

"You did that to me deliberately," she gasped, when she could talk again.

"Just an experiment," he said casually.

"I thought you wanted to take care of me and the baby, not upset me."

"You're not upset, lady, you're turned on—don't you know the difference?"

"So this was a test?" she said, rebuttoning her nightgown with trembling fingers.

"And you failed," he said, with a slight insinuating smile.

"Then you failed, too," Helene retorted, revamping her shattered defenses.

His expression changed, became guarded.

"Don't flatter yourself," he replied coldly.

"I'm not doing that," Helene said, striving for calm. "I may not have your vast experience of... of physical relationships, but even I know that what just happened between us was not typical."

"It was typical for me," he said cruelly.

"So you just felt like seducing me?" she asked, staring at him in disbelief.

"Sure," he said flippantly. "Why not?"

"Then what was all that talk about avoiding me because you have a secret?"

He turned away. "Whiskey rambling," he said dismissively. "You shouldn't pay so much attention to drunken drivel."

"*In vino veritas,*" she said.

"What the hell does that mean?"

"That people often tell the truth when they've been drinking," she fired back at him.

"Not me," he said, rounding on her with a leer. "It just makes me feel like stripping impostors of their pretenses."

"You promised me that you wouldn't touch me!" she burst out, stung by the unfairness of it.

"You wanted me to touch you," he said darkly. "Every day you've been in this house you've wanted me to touch you."

"You broke your word!" she insisted, dodging.

"I don't remember forcing you to do anything you didn't want to do," he countered, folding his arms and glaring at her.

"That's not the point!" she yelled. "You lied to me when you proposed marriage. You planned this all along."

"I did not!" he said heatedly, and it was the first thing he'd said that she believed.

"Then what?" she said softly, changing tactics, sensing that she was getting closer to an admission.

"Then nothing!" he exploded, taking a step toward her, his fists balled at his sides. "I don't have to explain myself to you."

"Then stay away from me!" she flung at him and ran into the hall, dashing for her bedroom as if it were a safe haven. She slammed the door and locked it, putting her back against it as if she expected him to break it down.

Nothing happened. She listened, her heart pounding, for any indications of movement, but the only thing she heard was her own ragged breathing.

Finally she lay down on her bed and waited for her heartbeat to return to normal.

It took a long time.

Chris remained in the living room, pouring himself another drink and then slumping disconsolately on the sofa.

Why did he feel like such a heel? He hadn't attempted rape, for God's sake. She had certainly consented to what he was doing; she had kissed him as if she were discovering passion for the first time and he had an uneasy feeling that she was. The only thing his "experiment" had proved was that he wanted her as desperately as he ever had, even more now that he had actually felt her eager, untutored response.

Was it possible that he was wrong about her? The thought kept surfacing, annoying him with its insistence, but he dismissed it once more with a vengeance. So what if Martin had been her only previous sexual experience? That did nothing to prove she hadn't been using his brother to solve her problems. In fact it made the whole scenario worse: she'd been planning to marry a man for whom she felt no desire, entering into a bloodless pact for mercenary reasons. She was just what he had always supposed and he'd better do exactly what she said and stay far away from her.

Because the next time he might not be able to stop.

"So you're not talking to him?" Maria de Salvo said, folding the last towel on top of the stack and handing the bundle to Helene.

"Who?" Helene said, putting the linens in the closet and shutting the door.

"Who do you think?" Maria said disgustedly. "Chris, that's who. The silence around here the last few days has been deafening."

"I don't want to talk to him. Or about him."

"So you're just going to let this go on indefinitely?"

"Maria," she said, sighing, "every conversation I have with him degenerates into a fight. What am I supposed to do?"

"You might try giving him a break."

Helene turned and faced her. "You too?" she said dryly.

"What do you mean?" Maria said.

"Martin was always telling me to give Chris a break. He was constantly making excuses for his brother."

"Perhaps because he knew more about Chris than you do," Maria said quietly.

"And you know too?" Helene asked.

"I know where he came from," Maria replied.

"So do I."

Maria shook her head. "You haven't seen it. You can't imagine where or with whom he lived."

"What does that have to do with his behavior toward me?" Helene asked angrily. She was getting tired of listening to reasonable people defend what she considered to be unreasonable behavior.

"A lot, I think. I don't guess he trusts women too much."

"Why?"

Maria ran her tongue over her lips. "Did Martin tell you about Chris's mother?"

"He said... he implied she was an alcoholic."

Maria nodded. "More than that, I'm afraid."

"What?"

"A loose woman, you might say."

Helene stared at her, appalled. "A prostitute?"

Maria shrugged. "Not formally, she didn't work in a brothel. But she did go with men for gifts and money."

"I thought... Chris said she used to be a maid here," Helene murmured, still trying to absorb it.

"She was, in the beginning. She was working in the house after Mr. Martin's mother died. Mr. Murdock, he was alone, and she was young and pretty."

"I get the picture," Helene said. "But why didn't she tell him about the child?"

"She discovered she was pregnant while Mr. Murdock was away on a long business trip. When he came back from it he was married."

"Oh."

"She was proud, you know?" Maria said.

Helene nodded. Having met the son, she could bet his mother was proud.

"She just went back to her people and had the baby. At first she took jobs, went from one thing to another, but there were always men and not the best kind... pretty soon they gave her things. She had a child to support and she took what she could get."

Helene looked away. It was all too easy to imagine.

"By the time Mr. Murdock divorced the second wife Chris was ten and his mother was well on her way down the wrong road. She took to the bottle and it killed her slowly. Can you imagine what it was like for the boy? This is a small town. Everybody knew his mother went with the migrants on payday, the traveling salesmen, the soldiers from the fort up north, anybody who had the price of a good time or a bauble to leave behind with her."

Helene was silent. She remembered Chris's remark about the empty chair on Father's Day at school. Apparently that had been far from the worst of it.

"And Chris stayed with her all those years?" she asked.

"He was only fifteen when she died," Maria replied.

"And then he found out who his father was."

"Yes. She never told Mr. Murdock because she was afraid he'd take Chris away from her. I guess she felt there was no reason to keep it quiet once she was gone and she wanted Chris to have his inheritance."

"How do you know all of this?"

"My older sister was a friend of the Quintanas, Chris's mother's family."

"I really wish I had known all of this earlier," Helene said thoughtfully.

"You can understand why Martin didn't tell you."

"Of course, but Chris can be so impossible a little background would have helped to explain him."

"I thought so."

"And that's why you're telling me now?"

Maria thought for a moment. "I want you to be patient with him," she finally said. "He has feelings for you."

"Violently negative ones," Helene said morosely. "He absolutely despises me."

"Not so," Maria said, shaking her head. "That's what he wants you to think."

"You're wrong, Maria."

Maria folded her arms resolutely. "You listen to me—I know him better than anybody. I have been working here since he first came to this house. He's trying to drive you away to protect himself."

"From what?"

"From you, his feelings for you. I saw what he felt, even back when Mr. Martin was alive."

Helene was incredulous.

Maria nodded. "Believe me on this. When you were here last June he was like a trapped animal. And now he is the same. He paced at night like a caged lion when you were sick."

At Helene's look of astonishment Maria added, "I was here, I heard it." She folded Helene's blue night-gown and handed it to her. "Don't you have a doctor's appointment this afternoon?"

"Yes, why?"

"I'll go with you and show you where Chris lived. Would you like to see it?"

"Very much," Helene said quietly.

Dr. Stern refilled Helene's prescription for mega-vitamins and told her to get plenty of rest. Maria was reading a magazine in the waiting room when Helene emerged from the office.

"What did he say?" Maria asked.

Helene told her.

"Chris will demand a report when I get back," Maria said, as they walked out to the parking lot.

"How do you know?"

"He always asks me about you. When he comes in from the ranch at night it's the first thing he does."

"Maybe he thinks I'm stealing the silverware."

"He's concerned about you."

"Then why doesn't he ask me himself?" Helene inquired despairingly. "He acts like I'm invisible and then checks on me behind my back. It's insane."

They got into Maria's car and Maria drove south from the office complex, past the strip mall and onto Main Street, which led to the old section of town. Once they crossed the tracks bisecting the industrial area they entered a part of town Helene had never seen. Dingy factories, some of them abandoned, and shabby row houses slumped toward one another in an attitude of resignation, their sloping roofs missing tarpaper tiles and their front porches sagging with the weight of disappointment and poverty. The streets were littered with rubbish, beer cans and broken toys abandoned by the skinny, dirty children chasing one another through scrubby empty lots sparkling with broken glass. Maria punched the door locks as they passed a gang of toughs drinking on a street corner and Helene shivered, glad that it was broad daylight.

"Here it is," Maria said quietly, slowing as they passed a wood-frame two-story building, its paint faded and peeling past the point of color identification. Its side was propped against a filthy brick structure next to it, which was boarded up but still sported a rusted metal sign that proclaimed Tyson Chemicals. The porch of the house was crumbling; slats from its splintered latticework were lying about on the cracked pavement and an entire step was missing. A plastic tricycle, its rear wheel dangling crazily, was overturned in a patch of weeds to the left of the front walk.

"This is where Chris lived?" Helene asked, swallowing.

"Yes. It was not quite as bad then. The neighborhood has degenerated a bit more since, but I'm sure this gives you an idea of what his childhood was like."

"He went from this to the Homestead?" Helene asked.

Maria nodded.

"That must have been quite a shock."

"I sometimes think he hasn't recovered from it yet," Maria answered, turning at the corner and heading back toward the shopping district, gunning the motor slightly.

"All right," Helene said, gazing out the window at their improving surroundings, "I understand that he had a tough life before he found his father and was accepted into the Murdock family. But why does he have to take it out on me?"

"Because he wants you, maybe more than anything else he's wanted in his life, but he's afraid to want—don't you see that? He spent the early part of his life never getting what he wanted. And to make matters worse, when he met you you belonged to his brother.''

"Martin is dead,'' Helene said dully.

"Yes, but think of the guilt involved! His brother, who took him in and helped him and accepted him as a member of the family—he's going to take that brother's girl? Not likely. Even now, it's eating at him all the time. I can see it.''

"Has he said any of this to you?''

"Of course not. Talking is not his thing.''

"Tell me about it,'' Helene said dryly. She looked over at the older woman. "Maria, I know you mean well, but I think you're dead wrong about his feelings for me. He treats me like a pariah—he hasn't spoken to me since...well, a good while. He seems very determined to pretend I don't exist.''

"He's lonely,'' Maria said.

"I can see why.''

"I've watched women pursuing him for years,'' Maria said, "ever since he came to the ranch, in fact. That Ginny Porter and a pack of others before her. He can't trust anybody enough to form a relationship. You've come the closest.''

"You've got to be kidding,'' Helene said, rolling her eyes.

"He asked you to marry him, didn't he?''

"He did that for the baby!'' Helene retorted.

"He did that for himself,'' Maria replied, slowing up for a red light. "I'm not saying he isn't interested in the child, but it was also the perfect excuse to bring you here."

"Why are you telling me all this now?" Helene asked, still unconvinced.

"I can see what's happening between the two of you and I'm so afraid that you'll give up on him and leave," Maria replied.

Helene said nothing. She had certainly been thinking about it.

"Look," Maria said, giving the car gas when the light turned green, "the rodeo is Saturday. Were you planning to go?"

"I didn't think Chris would want me there," Helene replied quietly, shrugging.

"Come with me," Maria said. "I'll pick you up and we'll go together, okay?"

"What about your husband?"

"He has to work."

"I'll go, if you don't tell Chris that we're planning to attend," Helene said.

"He knows I'll be there. I always go."

"Then don't say anything about me."

"All right," Maria answered. "If that's the way you want it."

"That's the way I want it," Helene said, and settled back against the seat as Maria headed out of town toward the ranch.

Martin had once said that September was the most beautiful month of the year in southern Wyoming and the day of the rodeo convinced Helene that he was right. The sun was bright, still retaining a shimmer of summer's heat, and the sky was a deep, cloudless blue, the color of gem topaz. The air was clean and fragrant and to Helene the pollution of the eastern cities she knew seemed far away. She and Maria parked in the crowded grass lot on the outskirts of the fairgrounds and then walked with the rest of the crowd to the grandstand, passing under huge banners that read "Twenty-fifth Annual Tri-County Rodeo." Food and soft-drink stands lined their path and the smells of hot dogs and barbecue and cotton candy mixed with the gamy odor of the animals stamping in the stalls nearby. They took their seats on a lower rung of the ascending wooden tiers and gazed down into the arena, where a clown was entertaining the onlookers, capering on the sawdust-covered floor while the participants prepared for the main events.

Helene had never been to a rodeo before and she was fascinated. The immense Brahma bulls, the bucking broncos, the courageous—foolhardy?—men who rode them, had her leaning forward eagerly in her seat. The caller who described the events under a canopy high up in the grandstand spoke so fast and in such specialized lingo that she could hardly follow what was going on, but the visual spectacle was enough to keep her riveted. After a break during which the clown entertained again and the crowd got up to visit the concessions, Maria tapped Helene's arm.

"Chris's event is coming now," she said.

"Is that Chris?" Helene asked, craning her neck at the rider who was ready in the stall, mounted, re-straining his restive horse with gloved hands.

Maria shook her head and pointed. "He's up last," she said.

Helene turned to see Chris, outfitted in chaps and jingling spurs, his hat shoved far back on his head with a red neckerchief tied at his throat, pacing in the packed dirt at the back of the stall. He was a study in concentration, hands on hips, staring at the ground.

"Look!" Maria said.

Helene turned back to the show as a calf was re-leased into the arena and seconds later a man burst forth from the stall, riding at top speed after it. With a coil of rope in his upraised hand, holding the reins with the other, he waited for the right second and then began to spin the lasso. As the calf dodged and spun, the cowboy released the rope with split-second timing and it whistled through the air, slipping around the animal as neatly as a pinball drops into a slot. The calf fell and the man was off the horse almost at the same moment, pinning it and wrapping its legs, then leap-ing up with his hands held high to show he was done. The crowd erupted into enthusiastic applause and the caller announced his time.

"Pretty good," Maria said judiciously. "Chris is going to have a hard time defending his title."

Several other men competed and then Helene heard "champion" and "Murdock" in the midst of the caller's babble, before his voice was swallowed up in a burst of thunderous screaming and clapping.

"There he is," Maria yelled triumphantly over the noise.

Helene watched as he tipped his hat at his reception, then replaced it on his head, settling back onto his horse and gathering the reins into his left hand. His rope was already looped over his shoulder and Helene felt the anticipation gathering around her as the crowd fell into an expectant hush.

Chris nodded and the calf burst from its stall onto the floor of the arena. Chris followed at lightning speed and the whole thing was over almost before Helene could comprehend it. She blinked and Chris was standing, the trussed calf at his feet, his arms thrust victoriously into the air. The people in the stands rose in one body and screamed their approval. She dimly heard the announcer caroling "winner and still champion" before the rest was drowned in a roar.

"Is this why you brought me here?" Helene yelled archly to Maria, who was chuckling wickedly.

"Aren't you impressed?" she yelled back.

Helene grinned and nodded.

They both watched as Chris walked to the center of the ring and swept his hat off his head, bowing deeply to the crowd.

"What a ham," Maria mouthed to Helene and they both laughed.

Chris's horse was led over to him and he mounted it easily, trotting slowly around the arena, his hat held aloft, his smile wide enough to be spotted from where Helene sat.

"What's this?" she asked.

"Victory lap," Maria replied.

"I've never seen him look happier," Helene said wistfully as the crowd noise abated.

"*That's* why I brought you here," Maria replied, shooting her a sidelong glance.

Chris was just heading back to the stall when a sudden series of loud popping noises erupted outside the corral fence, almost at his horse's feet. The horse reared and plunged and Chris, who had been holding the reins loosely with one hand, flew off the horse's back and landed at an awkward angle, facedown in the dirt.

There was a piercing scream and then a stunned silence as the clown and several of the wranglers rushed over to the sprawled figure on the ground.

"What is it?" Helene cried frantically.

"Some stupid kid with firecrackers," Maria replied angrily. "He scared the horse."

The caller tried to calm the crowd, which was switching gears from delighted approval to growing alarm as Chris didn't move. Finally there was sporadic clapping as he was carried off, a limp bundle supported by two cowboys, but Helene was close enough to see his lolling head and realize that he was still unconscious.

"Maria, we have to go down there," she said.

"Chris won't like it," Maria warned.

"I don't care. We have to see that he's all right." She was out of her seat and making her way down the aisle before Maria rose. The older woman shrugged and got up, following reluctantly.

The area around the changing tent was chaotic, but Helene pushed her way through the milling people until she located a man who was wearing a badge labeled Official pinned to his lapel.

"I have to see Chris Murdock," she said to him, as Maria stood uneasily at her side.

"You can't, miss. He's with the doctor."

"I'm his wife," Helene announced, as Maria closed her eyes.

"What?" the man said dumbly.

"You heard me."

"I didn't know he was married."

"Well, I'm telling you he is. Now are you going to let me in there to see him or not?"

The man took off his fedora and scratched his head.

"You got any identification?" he said doubtfully.

"Oh, for heaven's sake," Helene said in frustration, fumbling in her purse for her health-insurance card, which had been made out in the Murdock name. She thrust it under his nose. "How about this?"

He took it and examined it suspiciously, like an IRS agent perusing fraudulent tax forms. He shrugged and handed it back to her.

Helene sat down on an overturned packing crate and folded her arms. "I'm waiting right here until you go inside and check with the doctor. Will you please do that immediately?"

He looked from one woman to the other and decided that taking on such a formidable duo was not worth it. He made a disagreeable face and left. Helene saw him elbowing his way through the crowd and prayed silently that he was doing what she'd asked.

It seemed a very long time before he returned.

"Doc says you can go back there now," he said gruffly.

"I'll wait here," Maria said, stepping back.

Helene followed the man's broad back to the rear of the vast circus tent, which had been cordoned off to create a makeshift dressing area. She pushed aside a curtain and found herself standing ten feet away from Chris, who was sitting on the edge of a portable examination table, white surgical tape bisecting his brown midsection. He was sipping a beer as Ginny Porter applied an ice pack to the back of his neck.

"What are you doing here?" he greeted her.

"I was in the stands and saw you fall," she replied.

"I didn't know you were coming here today."

"Maria brought me."

"Well, you can go home," he said.

"Where's the doctor?" Helene inquired, looking around for him anxiously.

"He taped me up and left, said I was fine," Chris answered, not looking at her.

"Did he say you could drink that?" she inquired, nodding at the beer can.

"I don't need a mother," he said darkly.

"What about X rays? Didn't you hit your head? You were unconscious, weren't you?"

"You're a doctor too, now?" he said disgustedly.

"I'm taking him by the emergency room for some pictures on the way home," Ginny said. "He's not supposed to drive."

"That means you could have a concussion and you shouldn't be drinking liquor," Helene said.

"Go preach in church," he said darkly and took another big slug of his brew.

Suddenly out of patience with him, Helene rushed forward and knocked the can from his hand. He and Ginny stared at her in astonishment as the beer splattered all three of them.

"You are the most childish, immature individual it has ever been my misfortune to meet," Helene said flatly. "You should thank God that someone is concerned about you, instead of behaving like a spoiled four-year-old with a serious case of bad manners. I *will* go home, thank you very much, and if you start seeing double or throwing up or developing a headache I hope your little friend here has the good sense to admit you to the hospital once you get there. Goodbye."

She whirled on her heel and stalked out of the dressing room, signaling to Maria when she passed her.

"What on earth happened to you?" Maria asked, hurrying to fall into step beside Helene. "You smell like the brew that made Milwaukee famous."

"We had another fight—what do you think happened? I found him back there with his floozy, chugging beer and claiming that he was first in line for the president's physical fitness award.''

"So what upset you more, the beer or the floozy?'' Maria inquired mildly.

"Oh, shut up,'' Helene muttered, much too annoyed to rise meekly to the bait.

"Did you pour the beer on his head?''

"Almost.''

"What does that mean?''

"I knocked the can out of his hand and the contents sort of...splashed.''

"You?''

"All three of us.''

"You, Chris and the floozy?''

"Right.'' They had reached Maria's car and Helene yanked on the door handle impatiently as Maria unlocked her side.

"Which floozy was it?''

"Ginny Porter,'' Helene responded, flinging her purse into the back of the car with such force that it bounced wildly off the rear seat and onto the floor.

"She's been around a lot lately,'' Maria observed.

"I'd think she hadn't heard he was married, but I was there myself when she received the news,'' Helene said sarcastically, sliding onto the front seat next to Maria.

"It doesn't seem to have made much of an impression.''

"Apparently not.''

"Maybe he explained the situation to her," Maria said.

"I wish he would explain it to me," Helene muttered, and then added in an undertone, "Oh, I could kill him."

"Twenty minutes ago you were terrified that he *was* dead," Maria reminded her, starting the car.

"That was twenty minutes ago," Helene responded nonsensically, folding her arms in irritation.

Perceiving that rational conversation was not possible, Maria drove the car out of the lot, merging with the stream of departing traffic, and headed back to the ranch.

"Maybe I should come in and make sure you're all right," Ginny said, as they turned onto the winding drive that led up to the house.

"Just drop me off, Ginny, I'll be fine," Chris replied wearily, closing his eyes.

"But you shouldn't be alone," Ginny protested.

"I'm sure Helene is home by now."

Ginny fell silent. The subject of his quasi-wife was touchy and not one she wished to probe at the moment.

Chris stared grimly out at the night landscape. The moon cast an eerie spell on familiar objects; the paddocks and horse stalls and barns all seemed to glow with eldritch light. It was really very pretty, but he was in no mood to appreciate it; his ribs hurt and his head felt fragile and he couldn't dismiss Helene's impassioned lecture at the rodeo from his mind.

Helene had been genuinely worried about him; her expression when she burst in on him had been anxious, almost distracted. She was like a terrified parent who screams with relief at a formerly lost child; her fear had been replaced by anger once she saw that he was all right. And he had behaved badly, he knew that. He had been so stunned to see her that he covered his reaction with sarcasm, a coping mechanism that remained from his unhappy adolescence. Where she was concerned, he always said and did the wrong thing.

"What are going to do about your car?" Ginny asked, breaking the silence.

"I'll send Sam back for it tomorrow," Chris replied.

Ginny pulled up to the front door and got out, running around to take Chris's arm as he emerged from his door.

"I'm not an invalid," he snapped, snatching it back.

"I'm sorry," she said, chastened.

Chris sighed. She was only trying to help and it wasn't fair to take out his bad humor on her.

"No, I'm sorry," he said, shaking his head. "It was nice of you to bring me back and I do appreciate it. It's just that I'm tired and all I want is to get inside and go to bed. I'll call you."

Ginny had clearly hoped for more, but she would have to be satisfied with this farewell.

"Good night, Ginny, and thanks," Chris said with finality and headed for the door.

"Good night," she echoed and turned back to her car. He heard the motor fading down the drive as he entered the house.

He went into the kitchen to get a glass of water and found Helene at the table making out a list. She rose when she saw him and tried to walk past him, but he grabbed her wrist.

"Wait," he said.

She didn't move.

"What are you writing?" he asked.

"Things I'll need for the baby."

"A little early, aren't you?"

She shrugged. "It gives me something to do. Maria takes care of the housework and I'm not teaching, so..."

"So you're bored."

She tugged, but he held her fast. "I didn't say that," she replied uncomfortably.

"But you meant it," he persisted.

Helene gave up struggling, going limp in his grasp. "I'm not going to be drawn into another argument with you," she said simply. "Think what you want."

He let her go.

She tried to leave again, rubbing the wrist he had held with the fingers of her other hand.

"Please stay," he said.

She turned back to him. Had he actually said "please?"

"I want to apologize for what I said this afternoon," he began, his voice subdued.

Helene was riveted. A tornado would not have dislodged her from the spot.

"I didn't think you were coming to the rodeo, so I was surprised to see you," he continued.

She waited.

He shrugged. "I don't know why I said what I did, you just seem to bring out the worst in me. I've felt bad about it all night."

Helene felt her throat closing with emotion at the sincerity in his tone. His customary defenses were down, gone as if they had never existed.

"I'm just no damn good at this," he said huskily, making a helpless gesture.

"I thought you were doing very well," she said quietly.

"It isn't just tonight," he went on, clearly forcing the words to emerge. "Ever since you came here I've been behaving like a real jerk, telling myself that you were nothing but a fortune hunter. I could see once I got to know you that it wasn't true, but I couldn't seem to give up the idea."

"Why?" She could barely get the word past her lips.

"I'm not sure myself. Maybe because I have a hard time believing in people, maybe because you were Martin's girl and that still bothers me a lot. I know you slept with him first and the thought of that tears at my guts. I know I have no right, and maybe it doesn't make any sense, but that's how I feel."

Helene bit her lip, feeling perilously close to tears. She reached up and touched his face gently.

"You fool," she said softly, "the only reason I slept with Martin was because of you."

Five

———

"What do you mean?" he murmured, unmoving, his eyes fixed on her face.

Her hand fell and she turned away, trying to find exactly the right words.

"I loved Martin," she began, twisting her fingers together unconsciously. "I know I did, but there are all types of love. If I hadn't met you I probably would have never known the difference, never known what I was missing."

He was listening intently, his expression rapt.

"But I did meet you, and...you made me feel things I had never experienced before...and that was very upsetting. I felt disloyal to Martin. He was so good and honorable and kind. He deserved everything I had to give a man.''

He seemed to be holding his breath.

She inhaled deeply. ''I thought if I slept with him I could transfer those feelings to him.''

''And did you?''

She closed her eyes. ''I must have been a disappointment to Martin. I wanted to please him, but...''

''It wasn't like it is with us,'' he finished.

''No,'' she said in a tiny voice.

He reached her side in two strides and swept her greedily into his arms.

''Wait,'' she pleaded.

''No,'' he muttered, kissing the side of her neck. ''No more waiting. I've waited long enough.'' His lips traveled up to her cheek, then found her mouth. She kissed him back, losing herself for several long moments, then pushed him away, her palms against his chest.

''What?'' he said, his eyes heavy lidded, sultry.

''We have to think,'' she said desperately.

''Thinking is out,'' he replied. ''There's been too much damn thinking going on around here.'' He kissed her again.

Helene responded, giving up and relaxing against his shoulder. ''Then carry me,'' she whispered, when she could talk again.

''Pardon?'' he said, looking down at her.

''Carry me. I like it when you carry me.''

He picked her up and carried her down the hall to his room. When he kicked the door open, Helene

N IMPORTANT MESSAGE FROM THE EDITORS OF ILHOUETTE®

ear Reader,

ecause you've chosen to read one of our ine romance novels, we'd like to say thank you"! And, as a **special** way to hank you, we've selected <u>four more</u> of the ooks you love so well, **and** a Victorian icture Frame to send you absolutely **FREE!**

lease enjoy them with our compliments...

Luna Macro

Senior Editor,
Silhouette Desire

?.S. And <u>because</u> we value our ustomers, we've attached something xtra inside ...

PEEL OFF SEAL AND PLACE INSIDE

HOW TO VALIDATE
YOUR
EDITOR'S FREE GIFT
"THANK YOU"

1. Peel off gift seal from front cover. Place it in space provided at right. This automatically entitles you to receive four free books and a lovely pewter-finish Victorian picture frame.

2. Send back this card and you'll get brand-new Silhouette Desire® novels. These books have a cover price of $2.89 each, but they are yours to keep absolutely free.

3. There's no catch. You're under no obligation to buy anything. We charge nothing–ZERO–for your first shipment. And you don't have to make any minimum number of purchases–not even one!

4. The fact is thousands of readers enjoy receiving books by mail from the Silhouette Reader Service™ months before they're available in stores. They like the convenience of home delivery and they love our discount prices!

5. We hope that after receiving your free books you'll want to remain a subscriber. But the choice is yours–to continue or cancel, anytime at all!   So why not take us up on our invitation, with no risk of any kind. You'll be glad you did!

6. Don't forget to detach your FREE BOOKMARK. And remember...just for validating your Editor's Free Gift Offer, we'll send you FIVE MORE gifts, *ABSOLUTELY FREE!*

YOURS FREE!
This lovely Victorian pewter-finish miniature is perfect for displaying a treasured photograph– and it's yours **absolutely free**–*when you accept our no-risk offer!*

THE EDITOR'S "THANK YOU" FREE GIFTS INCLUDE:

▶ Four BRAND-NEW romance novels
▶ A pewter-finish Victorian picture frame

YES! I have placed my Editor's "thank you"
seal in the space provided above. Please send me 4
free books and a Victorian picture frame. I understand
I am under no obligation to purchase any books, as
explained on the back and on the opposite page.

(U-SIL-D-04/93) 225 CIS AH7M

_____

NAME

_____

ADDRESS   APT.

_____

CITY   STATE   ZIP

Thank you!

DETACH AND MAIL CARD TODAY!

THE SILHOUETTE READER SERVICE™: HERE'S HOW IT WORKS

Accepting free books puts you under no obligation to buy anything. You may keep the books and gift and return the shipping statement marked "cancel." If you do not cancel, about a month later we will send you 6 additional novels, and bill you just $2.24 each plus 25¢ delivery and applicable sales tax if any*. That's the complete price, and—compared to the cover price of $2.89 each—quite a bargain! You may cancel at any time, but if you choose to continue, every month we'll send you 6 more books, which you may either purchase at the discount price . . . or return at our expense and cancel your subscription.

BUSINESS REPLY MAIL
FIRST CLASS MAIL   PERMIT NO. 717   BUFFALO, NY

POSTAGE WILL BE PAID BY ADDRESSEE

SILHOUETTE READER SERVICE
3010 WALDEN AVE
PO BOX 1867
BUFFALO NY 14240-9952

NO POSTAGE
NECESSARY
IF MAILED
IN THE
UNITED STATES

lifted her head and said dreamily, "I always wanted to come in here."

"Why? Looking for girlie pictures on the walls?" He set her on the bed and then sprawled next to her, pulling her back into his arms. The only illumination came from the moonlight streaming through the window and across his striped spread.

"I was curious. About you." She hugged him back, feeling the thickness of adhesive tape on his ribs under his shirt.

"Nothing to know," he said lightly.

"Liar." She pushed aside his collar to put her face in the smooth hollow of his neck. "You just keep it all inside you."

He ran his hands up her back and pulled her blouse loose from her jeans. She shuddered when she felt his hands on her bare skin and clung to him tighter.

"Forget the first time," he said soothingly, aware of what she was thinking. "It was another life. Martin is gone and we can't bring him back, you're not betraying him. Nobody loved him more than I did and I believe it's the truth."

"I slept with him, knowing how I felt about you," she whispered, clutching his shirt.

"You didn't know then, it was only a guess. You had just met me." He stroked her hair. "Let it go."

"Is it wrong for me to be here with you?"

"Does it feel wrong?"

"It feels right," she sighed.

He turned her face up to his and kissed her again. "Then it is," he said, and she felt that it was.

The kiss deepened until she was straining against him and his breathing was harsh and irregular. He drew back to unbutton her blouse, the flush on his tanned cheeks deepened by the sun he had gotten that day at the rodeo.

"Does your chest hurt?" she asked, fingering his ribs through his shirt.

"Nothing hurts," he said, bending to tongue the silky valley between her breasts.

"But you fell . . ."

"I'm all right. You're not going to use that as an excuse to put me off tonight," he said, unhooking the front catch of her bra. He pushed the scraps of cloth aside and took her nipple into his mouth. She gasped and closed her eyes.

"Yes?" he murmured.

"Yes," she whimpered, holding his head against her.

He turned his attention to her other breast and she gripped him tighter, sinking her fingers into his thick hair. When he reached for the snap of her jeans she lifted her hips to help him.

He seemed to undress her in a second, her clothes flying off the bed and onto the floor. She was glad of the semidarkness and turned her face away when he loomed above her, staring at her.

"Helene," he said.

"Please, Chris. I'm shy."

"You're beautiful." He traced the curve of her hip with his hand. "Don't you know that?"

"I'm pregnant."

He dipped his hand inward and laid his palm against her belly. "You can't tell."

"Not yet."

"It will only make you more beautiful."

"I hope you think so when the only thing that fits me is a tent." She ran her hand up his sleeve. "I want to see you, too."

He smiled, his teeth a white flash in the dim light.

"Fair's fair," she said.

He stood and stripped off his shirt, the muscles of his arms and shoulders rippling with the movement. He tossed the shirt on a chair and unbuckled his belt, stepping out of his loafers at the same time. Helene watched as if in a trance, her eyes fixed on his shadowy but still-visible figure.

"You're beautiful, too," she said, when he was naked.

"I don't think I've ever been called that before," he replied, as he settled next to her on the bed. He drew her against him again and she gasped with the shock of feeling his lean, taut body all along the length of hers.

"Easy, now," he said, afraid that she would turn skittish at the last moment.

Helene clutched him, slipping her arms around his neck. He felt wonderful, his flesh firm and supple, smelling of shaving cream and saddle soap and the unique male essence that clung to all his clothes. When he felt her relaxing he slipped his hands beneath her hips and pressed her closer. She unconsciously adjusted her position to cradle him more fully and he groaned helplessly.

"You like that?" she whispered in his ear, sensing her power, feeling it grow within her, astonishing and new.

"God, yes," he said in a thick voice she hardly recognized.

"What else?" she asked, eager to learn.

"Anything you want—you can't be wrong," he replied, with a slight smile.

"This?" she said, pushing him back against the pillows, tracing his nipple with her tongue.

"You're a quick . . . study," he groaned.

She trailed a row of kisses down his abdomen, her movements awkward but fervent. When she got to his hips she hesitated, lifting her head.

"Don't stop now," he muttered hoarsely.

She reached down and took him in her hand and he closed his eyes, his breath coming in bursts.

"I've had such thoughts about you, touching you," she whispered. "Some nights I couldn't sleep, thinking about you just down the hall a few steps away."

"I know all about it," he said, surging upward and flipping her onto her back, then poising himself above her.

"Do you?"

"I've wanted for a long time to do this," he replied, bending to trail his tongue down her abdomen to the downy tuft at the apex of her thighs, imitating what she had done to him until she was digging her fingers into his scalp, trying to drag him upward.

"What do you want?" he said, raising his head.

"Come inside me," she begged. "Now."

He raised himself on his elbows and she ran her fingers down his back, now slick with sweat from his exertions. As he loomed above her she locked her legs around his hips, drawing him to her.

"Did this hurt—the last time?" he asked.

"A little," she said.

"I think you're ready now," he said.

"I am," she panted, impatient.

He entered her and she surged up to meet him; they both groaned aloud with the sensation.

"All right?" he gasped.

"Oh, yes."

He began to move within her, and she fell into his rhythm, a rhythm as old as time.

Helene woke in the predawn hours to find Chris lying next to her with his head propped on one hand, studying her.

"Hi," he said.

"Hi yourself."

"Feeling okay?"

"Spectacular."

"I thought so." He grinned. "You certainly didn't seem to be in any pain."

She punched him and he doubled up, faking a reaction. "I'll have you know you're pummeling an injured man."

"You weren't acting very injured."

"You can thank my marvelous recuperative powers." He pulled her into his arms and she lay back luxuriously against his shoulder. "I can't believe what a relief it is to just give in and do what I've wanted to do all along," he said seriously.

"All along?" she said.

"From the first moment I saw you."

"Me too." She gazed up at his clean profile, outlined against the moonlit window. "Why did you fight it so hard?"

"You mean after Martin was dead?"

She nodded.

He shrugged, and she saw him struggling to put his feelings into words. "I never had anybody special," he finally said. "Girls, sure, but nobody I felt so... strongly about, like you."

"Girls like Ginny?"

"I guess."

"I was very jealous of her."

"You were?" he said delighted. When she moved he added, "Please don't punch me again, I bruise very easily."

"I'll bet." She paused. "I thought you were sleeping with her and I couldn't stand it."

"I was."

Her heart sank.

"You were?" she asked feebly.

"Before I met you."

"And not since then?" Helene said happily.

"Nope."

"What did you tell her?"

"I told her I was married. You heard me, didn't you? You were there, as I recall."

"Then why has she been hanging around?"

"I guess I haven't been acting much like a blissful newlywed...."

"Hardly," Helene affirmed.

"And she could sense there was trouble."

"Very perceptive," Helene commented dryly.

"I think she was sort of sticking it out, to see which way the wind would blow."

"Have you known her a long time?" Helene persisted.

"Since we were kids."

"Did she live near you?"

"Down the block."

"She went to school with you?"

"Hey, what is this?" he asked, tipping her chin up with his forefinger and gazing into her eyes. "Are you working for the district attorney's office?"

She sighed. "That was my clever attempt to get some information about your past. All I know is what Martin told me, which wasn't much, and what Maria added since I married you, and that's not a lot more. You never talk about it."

He was silent a long time and then said, "I never talk about it because I'm trying to forget it."

"Was it that bad?" she asked gently.

"Before I came to the Homestead it was."

"Why?"

He sat up on the edge of the bed, pulling out of her grasp, and she felt a chill.

"Why dredge it all up now, Helene?" he said. "It's over and best forgotten."

When she didn't reply he sighed heavily and asked, "What do you want to know?"

"Well," she began, "Maria told me about your mother."

He swore under his breath.

"She meant well, Chris. She was only trying to help me understand you!" Helene protested.

"Trying to make you feel sorry for me, you mean," he said bitterly. "I don't need that."

"Of course not," Helene said, propping herself up against the pillows and drawing the sheet up to her chin. "Do you really think pity is what I feel for you?"

"I didn't want you to know," he said, ignoring her question, thrusting his hands through his hair in frustration. "You were engaged to Martin, for God's sake."

"What does that have to do with it?"

"His mother was some kind of damn socialite. She went to that school in Massachusetts, Mount Holly something...."

"Mount Holyoke?"

"Right, that one. And the second wife was always in the society columns, had an apartment in New York, used to go to those designer fashion shows—how does my history compare with that?"

"Martin didn't care."

"I wasn't in love with Martin," he said darkly.

Her heart went out to him. "Chris," she said gently, "my father was a convicted felon. Did you really think I would judge you on your parents' life? Where would I be if people judged me by mine?''

He shook his head vehemently; he saw a major difference and it was important to him that she understand. ''Your father was a white-collar type who got in over his head and thought a little creative financing would solve his problems. People understand that and wouldn't blame you for it.

''You can't tell me that's quite the same thing as having the town pushover for a mother.''

''Oh, Chris,'' she said sadly; it was clear she would never be able to overcome his lifetime of shame and disillusionment with the simple expedient of logic.

''See?'' he said. ''That's what I hate, that pitying tone.''

''That's compassion and you should know the difference.''

''There is no difference.''

Helene dropped the sheet and leaned forward, slipping her arms around his neck from behind and pulling him back toward her. ''Listen to me,'' she whispered in his ear.

''I'm listening,'' he said, turning to embrace her.

''I'm crazy about you, just as you are.''

''Is that right?'' he murmured indulgently, nibbling the shell of her ear.

''And I don't care how you got that way.''

''You don't care about any of it?'' he said, easing her back against the bed.

''No. I only wanted to know because I was trying to grasp why you were so defensive and secretive and...''

"Cranky?" he supplied.

"Cranky," she agreed, laughing.

"There was another reason," he said, bending to kiss her neck and then draw her to him.

"What?"

"Deprivation."

"I see."

"But we can remedy that," he added, moving on top of her and allowing her to feel his arousal.

"Let's," she said.

And they did.

When Helene woke again the sun was just coming up and she was shivering in the dawn chill. Chris was sprawled across her and as she moved his arm to get out of bed he said, "Whatimezit?"

"Six-thirty."

He groaned. "I have to break two horses today and it's a tough act on three hours' sleep."

"You should have thought about that before you spent half the night . . . doing what you were doing," she said, glancing in dismay at the pile of her wrinkled clothes on the floor. She went to his closet and rummaged quickly for a robe, which she slipped on; the sleeves tumbled over her wrists and she folded them back to her elbows.

"I wasn't doing it alone," he replied, grabbing her ankle as she walked past him.

"Chris?" she said.

"Yes?"

"Aren't you hungry?"

He grinned, tugging harder on her leg.

"For food."

He released her, rolling over heavily in mock disappointment and sighing loudly.

"I'm going to the kitchen, since I'm about to pass out from lack of nourishment," Helene said. "You're welcome to join me if you like, of course."

She heard indecipherable grumbling behind her as she went down the hall, but he appeared moments later as she was setting up the percolator, his hair rumpled and his eyes still heavy-lidded with sleep. He was barefoot but wearing his jeans, the snap unfastened at his waist. He dropped into a chair and slid down until he was resting on the base of his spine, his legs stretched out in front of him like a juvenile delinquent called to the principal's office.

"Is this your breakfast mode?" she asked him. "I don't believe I've witnessed this particular performance before today."

"I usually reserve it for Maria, while you're still sleeping," he said, yawning.

"Just think of what I've been missing," Helene said in a wondering tone. She retrieved the frying pan from the cabinet under the stove and added, "Scrambled eggs?"

"Anything," he replied.

"Gee, you're easily pleased at this hour."

"I'm too comatose to argue."

"I'll have to remember that." She got bread out of the box for toast and opened the refrigerator. "Orange juice?"

He made an unintelligible sound.

"I'll take that as a yes." When the coffee steamed she gave him a cup and left him in silence for several minutes while he drank it. She set a plate before him and waited until he looked up, draining his cup and blinking.

"Are you tracking yet?"

He nodded.

"You were awake enough when you were trying to entice me back into bed."

"That's different," he said grumpily, standing to refill his cup. He sat again and began to eat.

She stared at him.

"It's good," he said, glancing up at her.

"Thank you so much."

He ate industriously until his plate was empty and then he pushed it aside.

"Well?" she said.

"You look awfully cute in that robe."

"Don't let it give you any ideas."

"I've already got ideas." He pushed his chair back abruptly and came quickly to Helene's side of the table, bending to put his arms around her neck.

"Christopher."

"Yes?"

"I have to take a shower."

"I'll take one with you."

"What about your horses?"

"They can wait."

She got up, deftly eluding his grasp, and he trailed after her, catching hold of her robe cord. He pulled

her to him by its length, unraveling the tie and dropping it onto the floor.

"What are you doing?" she gasped.

"Isn't it obvious?" he answered, grabbing her.

She squealed and the robe slid off one shoulder.

The kitchen door opened and Maria stood on the
threshold, taking in the scene. Then she clasped her
hands to her breast and sighed dramatically.

"Don't tell me, let me guess," she said. "You two
kids are in love."

Six

"**K**nock it off, Maria," Chris said darkly, casting a sidelong glance at Helene and releasing her reluctantly.

"Chris said you were going to be late today," Helene muttered in embarrassment, hiking the robe up on her shoulder.

"I finished my errands early. What am I, punching a clock around here?" Maria replied, looking around in mute disapproval at her messy kitchen.

"I made breakfast," Helene volunteered unnecessarily.

"I see that," Maria said, starting to clear the table.

"Well," Chris announced, clearing his throat self-consciously, "I guess I'll get going." He pecked Helene on the cheek and headed down the hall to his room.

The two women looked at one another.

"Well," Maria said, setting a plate in the sink.

Helene grinned.

"What happened?" Maria asked, smiling too.

"I'm not quite sure myself. After I left the rodeo I thought he would never speak to me again, but when he came home he was...different. He apologized..."

Maria's eyes widened.

"...and really let me inside that shell for the first time, if you know what I mean."

Maria nodded.

"And then one thing led to another."

"I told you it would, eventually. He just had to fight it out with himself first."

"You do know him well."

"Not as well as you do, now," Maria replied mischievously, and Helene felt herself blushing.

"How do you feel?" Maria asked, adjusting the stream of water as she rinsed the plates.

"Happy, but afraid to hope for too much."

"He's happy too," Maria said.

"How could you tell? He was half asleep."

"I've never seen him looking so relaxed. Like he'd taken a big chance and won."

"I guess he did see it as taking a chance, but he was wrong. I'm so in love with him that it was no chance at all. He couldn't lose."

The object of their discussion reappeared, his hair damp from a quick shower, tucking his shirt into the waistband of his jeans.

"I'll come up to the house at lunch," he said, pressing Helene's shoulder as he passed. Then he stopped and confronted Maria, his hands on his hips.

"What are you looking at?" he asked, with mock severity.

"Not a thing," she answered innocently, taking a cup from Helene's hand.

Chris said something under his breath and vanished through the door. They heard him calling to one of the hands from the backyard, and then he started to whistle. They both listened to the sound of it fading into the distance.

"I haven't heard that for a long time," Maria said.

"I've never heard it," Helene replied.

"And just think, you're going to see him in the middle of the day. What a treat. For the last month he's been vanishing at dawn and materializing again at dark like a vampire."

Helene giggled.

Maria sighed, bending to load the dishwasher. "I don't know if I can stand this much happiness around here. This house has changed from a morgue to Happy Valley overnight."

"Thank God," Helene said fervently.

"Amen," Maria seconded, catching Helene's hand with her free one and squeezing hard.

"Maria," Helene said quietly, "I don't think I've told you how much your presence here has meant to me. Some days I thought I would go crazy without your sensible conversation and support.''

''Don't you get mushy on me now,'' Maria said briskly, releasing her hand. ''You told me you would help me wash those venetian blinds in the den, and you're not getting out of it.''

Helene laughed, and the two women went on companionably with their chores.

Maria went home at one o'clock, promising to return later in the afternoon, and Helene restrained herself until one-thirty before she went out to look for Chris. She checked her hair and makeup in the bathroom mirror and glanced ruefully at the straining waistband of her slacks. Then her impatience to see her husband—strange to think of him that way, but it was true—overcame her fading sense of propriety and she went trailing after him.

It was another gorgeous day and she enjoyed the walk out to the stables. The ranch hands—who never saw her—stared unabashedly as she passed, especially when she waved gaily to Sam, who was polishing a saddle outside the main barn.

''Have you seen Chris?'' she asked him, as he looked up at her and then nodded cordially.

''In there,'' he replied, jerking his thumb at the wooden structure behind him.

Helene walked around him and then slipped through the huge door, which was ajar. Inside the dim structure the horses were lined up in stalls, some snorting and shuffling, others contentedly munching hay and seemingly meditating. They reacted to her presence as she walked down the center aisle, the smells of manure and fresh hay and horseflesh overwhelming her. At the back, in an open area bordered by a tack wall studded with nails from which equipment dangled, Chris was rubbing down a weary looking horse.

"Hi," Helene said, suddenly feeling a little foolish, almost childish, for seeking him here.

He looked up and smiled, and her doubts vanished like a mist at sunrise.

"Is it that time already?" he said, glancing in dismay at his watch, which lay abandoned on a side table. He was stripped to the waist, his torso streaming with perspiration, his hair damp and matted.

"Almost two," she said.

"I'm sorry," he grunted, tossing aside the cloth he'd been using and wiping his forehead on the back of his arm. He smacked the horse's rump affectionately and the horse whinnied.

"Okay, okay, I get it. I know you're hungry," Chris said, leading the horse back to its stall. "We went a couple of good rounds this morning and he's not letting me forget he earned his lunch," he added in an aside to Helene. He settled the horse comfortably with its feed bag and water and then turned back to her.

"Did you miss me?" he asked, grinning, rubbing the back of his neck and his hair with a clean towel.

"Terribly. I finally came to look for you when it became clear you weren't going to show up. I think the hands were a little startled to see me wandering around like Apple Mary."

"They're just jealous," he said, tossing the towel into a corner and reaching for her. "Want me to rinse off at the pump out back?" he murmured, nuzzling her.

"No," she whispered, clutching him. His earthy smell, the product of hard work in the full sun, only made him more attractive. She slipped her arms around his waist and put her head on his shoulder. His skin there always startled her with its softness; today it still held the warmth of the sun and she snuggled against him shamelessly.

"Your body is so strong," she murmured. "I always feel that you could snap me like a twig."

"I have other, more pleasurable plans for you," he replied, amusement in his voice.

She looked up at him. "Did you always want me, from the beginning?" she asked.

"Always," he answered.

"Then why didn't you come up for lunch?" she demanded, pretending to pout. "I finally couldn't wait anymore."

"I really should have paid attention to the time," he said, rocking her slightly. "Are you mad at me?"

"Just kiss me and I'll forgive you," she said.

He complied, pulling her closer and sliding his hands under her sweater. Then he took her hand and led her into an empty stall, lifting her onto a pile of fresh hay that had been forked into it in readiness for a new horse.

"Stay there," he said.

"What are you doing?" Helene inquired, peering over the top of the stall. She watched him close the door of the barn and then drop the crossbar into place to prevent entrance. Outside, Sam looked up sharply at the sound and registered its meaning. He shook his head and grinned.

"Chris, for heaven's sake, everybody will know what we're doing in here!" Helene protested when he rejoined her.

"So what? The hell with them," he said amiably, flinging himself down next to her and reaching for her again.

"Can't we at least go up to the house?" she asked.

"Oh, and they're not going to figure that's a matinee?" he said, laughing, baffled by her logic. "Or maybe you just don't like the idea of the proverbial 'roll in the hay'?"

"I'm not that provincial," she said airily.

"No?" he countered, one eyebrow raised.

"No," she confirmed, seizing him and pulling him firmly down on top of her.

"Now this is more like it," he muttered, gasping as she pressed herself to him, fitting her curves to his lean, hard body. He lowered his head and kissed her throat, running his tongue down into the neck of her blouse, trying to unbutton it with clumsy, impatient fingers.

"Let me do it," she said.

"Why can't you just walk around naked all the time?" he asked. "It would be much easier."

"I don't think either one of us would get any work done," she replied, tossing her blouse aside.

"I can handle this," he said, reaching for her bra and popping the catch with his thumb. The lacy material caught in his hand and he bent to take her nipple in his mouth, pulling the bra off in the same motion. She held his head against her, closing her eyes, then turned his face up, bending to kiss him again.

"I love to kiss you," she whispered, overcome with emotion, stroking the soft hair at his nape.

He drew back to look at her. "Good," he said, smiling. "I love to kiss you too."

"No, you don't understand," she said, shaking her head. "Before, when we were always fighting, I wanted you so badly and couldn't do anything about it. I used to look at your mouth, your lips, and wonder what it would be like to kiss you."

He said nothing, staring at her, his expression serious.

"And then when I did, that first time, afterward I couldn't think about anything else."

He smiled slightly.

"I thought you were so beautiful. Your lower lip has a little dent in the middle, right here." She touched it with her tongue. "I wanted to feel it again, like this...." She kissed him and he took her fully in his arms, rolling her under him.

"I wish you had told me," he said, his face buried in the side of her neck.

"While you were insulting me?" she asked.

"I thought . . . oh, it doesn't matter now. I thought a lot of damn stupid things that really don't bear repeating," he said, his voice muffled against her.

"Forget about all that," she said soothingly. "It's over, it's in the past. Let's concentrate on now."

"I'm for that." He lifted up and unzipped her slacks, tugging them down her legs in one motion, then pulling his jeans off at almost the same moment.

"We've wasted too much time," he said tenderly, positioning himself above her.

"No more," she whispered.

"No more," he repeated as he entered her.

"I love you, Chris."

"Me too," he responded huskily, as the animals stirred and stamped around them.

"At some point I have to go back to work," he said some time later, rolling onto his back and throwing his arm across his eyes.

"Oh, can't we just stay in here forever?" she asked. "Wouldn't that be nice?"

"I think the hay would make you a little itchy after a while," he observed wryly, standing and looking around for his jeans. "And you might get hungry." He stepped into his pants and zipped them up, then combed his hair with his fingers.

"Be right back," he said and she heard him go out, then come back shortly afterward while she lolled in a state of sated lethargy.

"Are you planning to take a nap?" he asked when he returned. His hair was damp from the pump and he was buttoning the shirt he had retrieved from somewhere.

"Do you think the horses would mind?"

"Come on, lazybones, get up and get dressed. You're holding up the works."

She rose and fumbled into her clothes, remembering the sandwich she had stashed in her purse before leaving the house.

"I brought your lunch," she said, finding it in her bag and handing it to him.

"Thanks," he said shortly, his mind already on what he had to do that afternoon.

"What time will you be coming back to the house?" she asked, dusting the sticks of hay from her sleeves.

"Insatiable, aren't you?" he said, grinning.

"I was just wondering when to make dinner, for your information," she said piously.

"Isn't Maria coming back?"

"I was thinking about giving her the night off."

"Don't want any witnesses to the orgy?"

"Something like that," she conceded, trying not to smile.

"I'll be back at six," he said in a stage whisper.

"I'll be ready," she tossed over her shoulder, and she could hear him laughing behind her as she left the barn.

Sam was gone, but as she passed the paddock and started on the path up to the house she heard his voice calling out loudly behind her, "Mrs. Murdock."

She turned and saw him leading a pony past the corral.

"You have hay in your hair," he said.

She grinned, waved and ran up to the house.

A week of perfect bliss went by and at the end of it Helene found herself shopping for a dress. Chris had said that he wanted to take her back to the Spanish restaurant they'd visited with Martin—it was as if he wanted to exorcise his brother's ghost. At first Helene thought about objecting, but then she realized that for the rest of their lives they would be encountering things that reminded them of Martin. It was painful, but they had better start facing his loss now.

The clerk in the town's single ladies' boutique tried to be helpful, but nothing in Helene's former size fit and she finally settled on a pale blue dress one size larger. It had a blouson top, full skirt and elasticized waist. She didn't look bad, but she didn't look fantastic, either. Oh, well. Chris might as well get used to it. She was going to look this way and more so for some time.

She was standing in her slip when Chris came in from the ranch. He paused to kiss the back of her neck as he headed into the shower.

"Don't bother with a dress—you should go just like that," he said teasingly, catching her eye in the mirror.

"That would cause quite a stir in the restaurant," she replied, admiring his trim form as he disappeared through the door and into the bathroom.

By the time he emerged in a cloud of steam, she was ready. He dressed quickly in pearl gray raw silk slacks with a charcoal gray sweater, banded at the neck and cuffs with a wide navy stripe—he seemed to know instinctively what colors looked best on him. For a man who devoted no time to shopping or clothes, when he departed from his customary jeans he always looked just right, not fashion conscious, just simple and masculine—sensational. Helene sighed inwardly. It was going to be some job keeping up with him, but then again, she didn't want anyone else to fill the position.

"What are you thinking?" he asked, putting his wallet and keys in his pocket.

"Why?" she asked, startled.

"You looked worried. Is something wrong?"

"Not a thing," she said, smiling back.

He stretched out his hand and she took it. "Good," he said. "I want you to have a nice time tonight."

"How can I not have a nice time?" she inquired, moving into the protective curve of his arm. "I'm with you."

Once they got to the restaurant, however, she understood why he had been concerned. They were led to a small secluded room, where a round table was laid with an ivory linen tablecloth and set with heavily carved silver and delicate, dazzling crystal. Their own private waiter was standing ready with a snowy napkin folded over his arm, and a huge bouquet of camellias and carnations sat on a sideboard, adding a lovely perfume to the ambience.

"Did you arrange all this?" Helene asked dazedly, taken aback by the elaborate preparations.

"No," he said seriously, "my best information is that the tooth fairy did it."

"Chris, I . . ." she swallowed. "It's such a beautiful surprise. Thank you."

He smiled, as pleased as a six-year-old who had made a birthday present at camp.

The waiter approached them and held out a chair for Helene. She sank into it, noticing her own reflection in the shining dinner plate. When Chris sat opposite her he said to the waiter, "Bring a pitcher of sangria, *por favor.*"

"And some mineral water for me," Helene added.

"Oh, that's right, I forgot. No booze for you." He picked up a sheet of paper next to her place setting and handed it to her.

"What's this?" she asked.

"Your menu."

"What happened to the regular one?"

"I designed this specially for us."

"It's all in Spanish."

"Very observant. I'll translate."

There was a silence.

"Well?" she said impatiently.

"Chorizos for an appetizer. That's Spanish sausage with peas and corn."

"Okay. What else?"

"Langostinos in garlic sauce."

"Oh-oh."

"We'll breathe on each other."

"What's a langostino?"

"Kind of a cross between a big shrimp and a small lobster."

"Sounds good."

"And for the main course—*mariscada*."

"What's that?"

"You'll see."

"It's not like snails or eels or anything like that, is it?"

"I promise it's not, you'll like it."

The waiter then brought their drinks and the food followed shortly afterward. Helene had to admit that everything was wonderful. Chris had obviously taken a lot of time and care in planning this meal and she loved him for it. They were having dessert, a delicate flan smothered in caramel sauce, when Chris produced a blue velvet jeweler's box from his pocket with a flourish.

"What's that?" Helene asked, her cup of herbal tea halfway to her mouth.

"A surprise," he replied.

"Another one?"

"Open it."

Helene took the box and looked at him curiously as she pressed the hinge. The top lifted to reveal a band of gold studded with diamonds set on a bed of white satin.

"It's a ring," she said.

"Very astute."

"For me?"

"No, it's for Maria. I'm just showing it to you to hear your opinion on it before I give it to her," he said dryly.

"I'm sorry. I guess I must sound stupid. I just wasn't expecting anything like this."

"Well, it was a little late for an engagement ring, so I thought a wedding ring would be a better idea. I got a plain one for me, too. I want us to have a real wedding soon, in church. Okay?"

"Okay," she breathed, feeling the sting of tears behind her eyes. Please don't let me cry, she thought.

"Are you all right?" he asked gently.

"Yes, I'm just so happy," she said, wiping her eyes with her napkin.

"How did you know what size?"

"I took a ring from your jewelry box with me, and then replaced it that night. You never missed it. Try it on."

Helene removed the ring from the box and slipped it onto her finger. She had to push it past the knuckle.

"Too small?" he said anxiously.

"No, my fingers swell a little at the end of the day. It's the pregnancy. After the baby comes it will fit fine."

He nodded.

"More coffee?" the waiter said at Chris's elbow.

"Thanks." The waiter refilled his cup and then departed unobtrusively.

"They certainly treat you like royalty in this place. How do you rate it?" Helene asked.

"The owner is a relative of my mother's."

"But I thought they were all..." she stopped.

"Poor?" he suggested.

"Yes," she said in a small voice.

"I gave him the money to get the place started eight years ago, after I was making a good profit on the ranch. Let's just say he's been very grateful."

"You mean you're a part-owner here?"

"No, I just gave him a loan which he later repaid. I didn't ask for any interest. But he has a long memory."

"You're a good person, do you know that?"

"Please," he said, looking away, embarrassed.

"I think it was your way of remembering your mother," Helene said gently.

"Don't get started on that again," he said.

"Chris, we don't love people because they're perfect—you must know that. You obviously loved your mother, no matter what kind of problems she had."

He said nothing, his face pensive.

"I tried to hate my father after he brought our whole world crashing down about our ears, but I found I just couldn't do it."

"Would it surprise you to learn that my capacity for hate was greater than yours?" he asked evenly.

Helene met his intense dark eyes and found herself saying, "No, it wouldn't surprise me."

"Then don't judge me by your reactions. She ruined my life. I was glad when she died."

"Maybe so, but you didn't hate her."

"I hated her life. I think she did too."

"That's not the same thing."

"Don't play word games with me, Helene," he said testily, fiddling with the saltshaker.

"Chris, I don't want to ruin this lovely evening, but I can't have a relationship with someone who constantly shuts me out every time a painful subject comes up. Can you understand that?"

He sighed, eyeing her warily.

"Do you want me to be one of those toy wives who just talks about the weather and decorating the den and what's for dinner? I want to really help you, be with you, face everything with you. Isn't that what you want too?"

There was a long pause, then he nodded slowly.

"Then answer one question for me. Why didn't she ever tell you who your father was?"

"She was afraid I would leave her if I knew I had a better place to go. She put it in her will because then she would already be dead and it wouldn't matter."

"Are you sure?"

He nodded. "She was terrified of being alone. The men she went with, well, they were never good for more than a few days, a week. I was the only constant in her life."

"Would you have left if you had known earlier?"

He thought about it, then shook his head. "I don't know."

"It's a shame, Chris. With your father's help you might have been able to do something for her."

He nodded. "I've thought about that many times."

The waiter came back and Chris asked for the check. When he was told there was no charge, he threw up his hands.

"Tell Jorge I'll be in touch," he said to the waiter, who smiled and left.

"I don't come here as often as I would like, because Jorge always does this and I feel like I'm taking advantage of him," Chris said, as he pulled out Helene's chair.

They made the drive back in a shared, comfortable silence; Helene had never felt so close to him. They walked through the door and Chris said, "Ready for bed?"

"Yes."

"But not for sleep."

"No."

He nodded, his eyes locking with hers.

They walked hand in hand down the hall to his room and closed the door behind them.

"Why do we sleep in here?" Helene asked, as she stretched to pull down the zipper at the back of her dress.

"The bed's bigger?" he suggested.

"I think it gives me an illicit thrill to be running back and forth between bedrooms," she said, laughing.

"How can it be illicit?" he asked, pulling his shirt-tails out of his pants. "We're married."

"It feels illicit."

"That's because you're having a good time," he said, standing behind her and bending to kiss the back of her neck.

"Very true," she replied, closing her eyes.

He pulled her dress off her arms and she stepped out of it as it fell. His hands slipped down to her hips and he arched himself against her.

"A perfect fit," he murmured in her ear.

Helene sighed as she felt his arousal and he dropped his head to her bare shoulder. His mouth moved along her bare back, the friction of his tongue against her skin causing her knees to weaken.

"Helene?" he said, sliding his hands under her arms and enclosing her breasts, his voice muffled by her flesh. He stroked her nipples with his thumbs, teasing them into peaks as she moaned helplessly.

"Yes," she whispered, turning to face him, lifting her mouth for his kiss.

He responded instantly and she opened her lips under his, welcoming the invasion of his tongue. She ran her palms over the hard surface of his back, pushing aside the folds of his loosened shirt. He put his hands on either side of her waist and lifted her, setting her on the bed. He stripped off their remaining clothes and then fell with her full length, pulling her tight against him again.

"Each time I'm with you I'm afraid it will be the last," she said, burying her face against the smooth expanse of his shoulder.

He held her off to look at her.

"Don't talk like that," he said sternly.

Helene reached up and tangled her fingers in his hair, the silky strands slipping through her grasp, and then dug her nails gently into his scalp.

"I guess I can't believe you're really mine," she whispered.

He grunted and shifted position, adjusting himself so she could feel him more fully.

"I really am," he replied.

Helene wrapped her legs around his hips, her eagerness inflaming him. He kissed her again, so intensely that she thrust against him restlessly, muttering something he couldn't understand.

"What do you want?" he said, his lips against hers, his tone low and sensuous.

"You," she said. "Now."

He gave her what she wanted.

"I'm hungry," Helene said.

"I'm not surprised. You ate almost nothing at dinner."

"I was excited."

"Honey, that wasn't excited. Excited is what we just had here in this bed."

Helene punched him. Lightly.

"Ow," he said, unconvincingly.

"I sure wish somebody would get up and make me a sandwich," Helene announced.

Silence thundered through the room.

"I had such a big night, the ring and everything," she added hopefully.

There was a slight rustling of sheets, some thumping of pillows, but no verbal response.

"I am pregnant, after all," she said dramatically, pulling out her trump card.

"Oh, all right," he replied, sighing loudly and shifting in the bed. She heard his feet hit the floor and then the lamp on the bedside table snapped on, shedding a buttery glow across the spread.

"Turkey with lettuce and tomato on a hard roll," Helene said with satisfaction.

He glanced at her over his shoulder. "This is not Joe's deli," he replied. "You'll have to take what's there."

"I bought all of that myself yesterday," Helene said smugly.

"For just such an emergency," he said, pulling on his pants.

"You never know," she said, grinning.

"Apparently, you do," he replied pointedly, laughing as he padded into the hall.

"Don't use the roll if it's stale. There's whole-wheat bread in the keeper," she called after him.

He stuck his head back into the bedroom. "Anything else? How about a fresh rose on the tray?"

"That would be a nice touch," she offered brightly. "And don't forget the mayonnaise."

"On the rose?"

"On the sandwich, wise guy."

"I'll see what I can do," he said dryly, and she listened contentedly to his progress down the hall and then heard the squeak of the refrigerator door. She propped several pillows against the headboard and sat back against them comfortably, drawing the sheet up under her arms and smoothing the spread across her lap. She relaxed, closing her eyes, and was almost asleep by the time he came back.

"Wake up," he announced as he came through the door. "If I made this masterpiece at two in the morning you are going to eat it."

Helene blinked and straightened. "Looks great," she said.

"It looks like I hacked the roll in half with a machete," he said apologetically, "but I did the best I could."

Helene surveyed the plate, which bore what might have been the remains of a kaiser roll stuffed with what resembled a wilted day-old salad. She picked it up gingerly.

"How does it taste?" he asked doubtfully, as she took a bite.

"Yum," she said, truthfully. It tasted a lot better than it looked. She chewed enthusiastically.

"Well, anyway, it's food," he said, sighing and climbing in next to her. He popped the top of the can of beer he had brought for himself and handed her a glass of seltzer.

"Thank you," Helene said tenderly.

"You're welcome." He rolled onto his side, watching her eat.

"Want a bite?" she asked, proffering the ragged roll.

"No, thanks. I killed it, I'm not going to eat it too."

Helene giggled and then hiccuped loudly.

"Oh, no. Not again," she said, gasping for air. She put the plate on the floor and tried to hold her breath, but she hiccuped once more.

"You know what the doctor said," Chris reminded her. "It's the baby pressing on your diaphragm. Just relax and breathe normally."

Helene relaxed, took a deep breath, then hiccuped twice.

He sighed and pressed her flat onto the mattress. "Close your eyes," he instructed.

Helene did so.

"Close your mouth and exhale through your nose," he said.

She obeyed.

"Now let your arms and legs go limp," he intoned.

Helene felt all her muscles go slack.

He peeled the sheet back from her torso and took one of her nipples in his mouth.

"Hey," she said, sitting up.

"Cured your hiccups, didn't it?" he asked.

Seven

"What do you want to do tonight?" Helene asked, as they were finishing dinner the following evening.

Chris looked at her and grinned lasciviously.

"Besides that," she said.

He shrugged.

"Can we go to Brodie's?" she asked.

"Why do you want to go there?"

"Just to see it."

"It's not a place for you," he said shortly.

"Why not?" Helene demanded. "Is it the national headquarters for Murder, Incorporated?"

"It's a beer joint, Helene, you won't be meeting a lot of first-grade teachers there."

"Maybe that's why I want to go."

"Expanding your horizons?"

"Possibly. You spent a lot of time there. Are you trying to hide your past from me?"

He narrowed his eyes at her. "Playing district attorney again?"

"I suppose I can always go by myself," she said airily.

"You're not going there by yourself," he said firmly.

"Well?" she countered.

"All right." He ran his glance over her outfit. "You'll have to change your clothes," he said.

She looked down at her skirt and blouse, sheer hose, dark pumps. "What's wrong with my clothes?" she asked.

"You look like you're about to give a lecture on the difference between hard and soft *g*."

"I thought you liked the way I look," Helene said softly, suddenly feeling hurt.

Chris put down his coffee cup and slid out of his chair, coming to stand behind her at the sink.

"I love the way you look," he said, pushing her hair aside to kiss the back of her neck. "But it will make you stand out like a reindeer in the Easter parade at Brodie's Bar and Grille."

"Then what should I wear?" she asked, turning around and into his waiting arms.

"Jeans and a T-shirt. Boots."

"I don't have any boots."

"Tennis shoes, then."

"You mean sneakers? That's what we call them in New Jersey, sneakers."

"Right." He kissed the tip of her nose. "Go put on your sneakers and I'll take you to Brodie's."

Helene hurried to change and reappeared in the kitchen minutes later, wearing her oldest jeans with a leather belt and a faded cotton shirt tucked into it.

"There you go," Chris said, when he saw her. "Perfect."

"I don't feel perfect. I had to let the belt out two notches and the top of my jeans won't button closed."

"Gee, you look like you've gained at least . . . two ounces."

"Three pounds," she said glumly.

"My, my, what's next? Weight Watchers? Come on, chubby, your chariot awaits."

Brodie's was in the same section of downtown as the house Chris had shared with his mother, on a dark corner across the street from a defunct convenience store with Spanish-language signs tacked to its front. Neon advertisements glowed in Brodie's windows and country-and-western music blared from the smoky interior as they pushed their way through double doors and went inside.

The main room was dominated by a wraparound bar, with most of the stools occupied by customers, and a group of pool tables with a clutch of booths at the back. Through an alcove at the left dancers moved to the music of a jukebox just inside the door. Voices called out greetings to Chris as they entered, and he nodded to several people as he steered Helene past the bar toward one of the tables. Once they were seated a waitress appeared almost immediately.

"Hi, Chris, how ya doin'?" she asked brightly as Jimmy Buffet's "Margaritaville" began to pulse through the room.

"Hi, Marge," Chris replied.

"Two beers?" Marge said.

"Mineral water for me," Helene said.

"Mineral water?" Marge said, looking at Chris.

"You have club soda, don't you?" Chris asked.

"Sure."

"Beer for me and club soda for the lady."

"This must be your wife," Marge said, examining Helene with a practiced eye.

"That's right."

"Ginny told me you got married."

There was a long, pregnant pause.

"I'm awfully thirsty, Marge," Chris said gently.

"Right," Marge said, and walked away.

"I'm beginning to think that you knew best about my coming here," Helene observed quietly.

"Don't pay any attention to her," Chris said.

"Did you see the way she was looking at me? I'm sure Ginny can expect a full report at the earliest opportunity."

"Ginny has already seen you."

"Then they'll compare notes."

"Are you really that insecure? Is that why you wanted to come here?"

"Let's put it this way. I realize that I'm something of a departure from your previous life and I have been curious about what you were doing before you met me."

"I was doing nothing before I met you. My life began the first time I saw your face," he said quietly.

Helene reached for his hand across the table, her eyes filling with tears. Every time she began to panic about the differences between them, the chance she had taken in falling in love with him, he said something like that and her fears dissolved like morning mist.

"How about a game, Chris?" said a voice at her elbow.

She looked around to see a middle-aged man, suntanned and weather-beaten, gazing at Chris expectantly.

"I don't know, Chet. I'm here with the lady," Chris replied, smiling slightly.

"Oh, it's all right with me," Helene said hastily.

"This the missus?" Chet asked.

"That's the missus," Chris confirmed.

"Ma'am," Chet said, inclining his head and extending a callused hand. "Right proud to meet you."

Helene shook hands with him, her fingers soft and small against his horny palm.

"This is Chet Ridgemont, Helene. Chet works on the Simpson ranch over in Red Pass," Chris said.

"Pretty filly," Chet said to Chris.

"Thanks," Chris said shortly, glancing at Helene. She felt she had passed some sort of test.

"Dance?" Chet said to her.

"I'm afraid I don't know how to do that," Helene said, glancing at the couples doing the two-step in the next room.

"It's easy, I'll show you," Chet said.

"I think she's a little tired tonight, Chet, maybe some other time," Chris intervened.

"That's right. Go ahead and have your game," Helene said. "I'll just relax and listen to the music."

"Why don't you get a table, Chet? I'll be right along in a minute," Chris said.

Chet nodded to Helene and moved off to the side of the room, where he was soon selecting a cue and chalking it.

"Can't you do the two-step, Mrs. Murdock?" Chris said to Helene as he rose.

"It didn't come up much in New Jersey," Helene replied.

"You'll have to learn if you plan to stay out here," he said.

"Some other time."

"Sure you'll be okay alone?" he asked.

She nodded and regretted it shortly, as Marge slid into the seat across from her as soon as Chris was gone.

"Here's your drinks," Marge said, depositing a club soda in front of Helene and slipping a paper coaster under Chris's beer.

"Thank you," Helene said pointedly, taking a sip of her drink and turning away.

"Not from around here, are you?" Marge said.

"No."

"Back East?"

"Yes."

"I thought so—you talk kinda funny. Like those people on TV giving out the evening news, you know what I mean?"

Helene didn't know what to reply to that, so she just smiled and took another sip of her drink.

"So how long you been out here?" Marge went on.

"Not long," Helene answered, thinking glumly that she had brought this interrogation on herself by insisting on coming here.

"Me, I never thought Chris would get married," Marge volunteered. "He was always such a free spirit, took his good times where he could find them. It seemed like he just lived for that ranch and the rodeo. All those trophies in that case against the wall are his, you know."

"They are?" Helene asked in surprise, wondering what else she didn't know about her husband.

Marge nodded. "Chris didn't want them and Brodie said they'd be good for business, the champ bein' a regular customer and all."

Helene glanced over at Chris, who was leaning across a pool table angling for a shot.

"Think you'll be staying out here?" Marge inquired.

"I imagine so. Chris wouldn't want to leave the ranch."

"Marge, you got some thirsty people looking for you back at the bar," said a voice to their left.

Both women looked up to see a heavily muscled blonde in his late thirties grinning down at them. He had his short sleeves rolled up to expose bulging biceps and a pack of cigarettes tucked into his sagging breast pocket. His smile revealed a broken incisor and did not extend to his hard blue eyes.

"All right, Randy," Marge said meekly, sliding out of the booth and scurrying back to the bar.

Randy took her place, still grinning. "I'm Randy Sills—I work here nights. Keeping order, you might say."

"Are you the bouncer?" Helene asked bluntly, before she could stop herself.

"That's right. And you're the Murdock bride. Been hearin' a lot about you from Sam. Your husband's headman is my uncle."

"I see." Helene looked nervously over at Chris, who was leaning on his cue watching Chet take a shot.

"So which brother is it you're hooked up with, exactly? I keep forgettin'. You were engaged to the dead one and now you're married to the live one, is that the story?"

"That's it," Helene said coldly, now actively trying to catch her husband's eye.

"Quite a switch, huh? I mean I never met the older one but Sam says he was just the opposite to our boy Chris—must have taken some gettin' used to, right?"

Chris finally looked up from his game and saw Helene staring at him. He dropped his cue without even glancing at it and it slid off the corner of the table and hit the floor.

"Hi, honey," Helene said loudly, reaching out to take his hand and smiling warmly when he arrived.

"Sills," Chris said flatly in acknowledgement of the other man, his eyes wary.

"Hiya, Murdock. I was just havin' a little chat with your wife," Randy said.

Chris nodded, unconvinced. His wife looked too stressed for that to be the whole story.

Randy rose and slid out of the booth, turning until he was facing Chris in the aisle.

"She was just about to tell me what it was like to go from your brother to you. Like one of them what do you call 'em, those lady slaves."

"Chris, let's leave," Helene said quickly, getting up and tugging on his arm. She was too aware of what the tightening of his jaw meant to wait for the rest.

"Watch it, Randy, your brains are running out of your mouth," Chris said quietly. Too quietly.

"Yeah, well, at least I'm not the type to steal my brother's woman. Hardly waited for the body to get cold before you jumped the fiancée, right, boy?"

Chris lunged forward and his fist crashed into Randy's jaw before anyone could prevent it. Helene gasped in horror as Randy staggered back, shaking his head, then recovered enough to launch himself at Chris.

The scene that followed seem to linger in slow-motion limbo forever, but Helene realized afterward that it probably lasted only a few seconds. The two men struggled, tumbling to the floor and knocking over a hat stand, rolling over and over and landing wild punches before Chet and several others succeeded in prying them apart.

"You're a sore loser, Sills—you were a sore loser in the third grade," Chris gasped, struggling against the arms holding him back, trying to get at Randy once more.

"And you were a low-life townie then and you still are now, Murdock," Randy replied through bloody lips. He had gotten the worst of the fight and looked it. "A hundred rancher fathers and lawyer brothers can't change that."

Two of the men dragged Randy off to the next room and Chris slumped back into the booth they had left, taking a long pull of his now flat beer. Helene stood mute, staring at the large, purpling bruise on his left temple.

"What are you looking at?" he finally said.

"Are you all right?" she said, finding her voice.

"Of course, I'm all right. That's not the first fight I've ever had and it won't be the last."

"Why?" she said, sitting across from him. "Why was he acting like that?"

"He came in second at the rodeo. He comes in second every year—I beat him all the time. I guess he doesn't like it."

"What was all that about third grade?"

"We hated each other as kids, too. This is nothing new. We lived near each other and he resented it when I found my family and took over the ranch. He's still living in the same house and thinks I'm putting on airs. I don't give a damn what he thinks, to tell you the truth, but saying that about you got my goat.''

"That's why he said it.''

"Sam can't see what a loser he is. Randy is his brother's kid and Sam talks too much around him.''

"It isn't Sam's fault. I wanted to come here.''

"I guess you didn't know that Randy Sills has the emotional development of a two-year-old.''

"You didn't look too highly evolved yourself, rolling around in the sawdust with him.''

Chris looked at her for a long moment, then glanced away.

Marge appeared with a bunch of ice wrapped in a towel.

"For your eye,'' she said to Chris, handing the bundle to him.

Chris applied the pack gingerly to his face, wincing slightly.

"Randy's face is much worse,'' she volunteered.

"Randy's face was much worse before the fight,'' Helene said, after Marge left. "Poor Marge. She must have nursed a few gladiators before you two.''

"Especially on Saturday night, there's always at least two real dustups.''

"Aren't we fortunate it isn't Saturday?'' Helene asked sweetly.

"Have you seen enough of Brodie's?'' Chris asked dryly, setting the ice pack on the table.

"I think so,'' Helene replied.

"Then how about we head home?'' he asked.

"Fine.''

They walked out, Chris's arm around her protectively, saying goodbye to Chet and Marge at the bar.

"Do you want me to drive?" Helene asked as they neared the car and his hand went into his pocket for his keys.

He looked at her in disbelief, the neon window lighting making his skin glow red.

"Chris, you just had a concussion at the rodeo and now you had this fight. Are you sure you're okay to drive?"

"I'll tell you about it when I'm not," he said shortly, opening her door for her.

Helene sat back against her seat wearily and closed her eyes, wondering if the day would ever come when he could admit that he wasn't a superman.

He got in and drove away, negotiating the trip in silence for a while before he said, "Are you mad at me?"

"No."

"Then what? There's a draft of cold air drifting toward me from your direction."

"I'm just realizing that living with you will require some . . . adjustments."

"To dealing with low-life trash, you mean?"

"I didn't say that."

"You were thinking it."

"You can't possibly know what I was thinking."

"Then tell me," he said challengingly.

"I was thinking that you must have survived some tough knocks to get where you are," she said honestly.

"And where am I? Living off a business my father started and my brother nurtured, in love with a woman who thinks my friends are lowlifes and just had to see my old hangout to prove it to herself." His voice was bitter, his profile stony in the near dark.

"Stop the car," Helene said.

"What?" His head turned.

"I said pull over and stop the car."

"Helene, I'm in the middle of Converse Street."

"Then turn off Converse Street, I want to talk to you."

Sighing loudly, he did as she asked, turning into a residential block and gliding to a stop at the curb. He switched off the ignition and said, "Well?"

Helene slid across the front of the car as far as the bucket seats would allow and put her arms around his neck.

"What's this?" he murmured, leaning in close to her.

"I'm kissing you," she said, doing just that.

He kissed her back.

"I wanted to see Brodie's because I'm trying to understand you," she said, her lips against his cheek, roughened now with evening shadow. "All of this has happened so fast that I feel at a loss. I wasn't trying to embarrass you or show you up. I thought it would bring us closer if I could share some of your past with you."

"It's not going to bring us closer for you to watch me fighting with Randy Sills," he replied, kissing her neck. "I saw your face. You were horrified."

"That's just because I never saw a fistfight before, except in the movies. I've led a sheltered life—you said so yourself."

"I assumed it was because you thought I was a thug."

"Of course I don't think that," she said, putting her head on his shoulder.

"Helene, I'm trying to change, but it's not about to happen overnight. And going back to places like Brodie's isn't going to make it any easier on me."

"No more Brodie's, I promise," Helene whispered, pressing closer to him.

A police car came down the street and slowed as it cruised past them.

"We'd better get a move on before we're arrested," Chris said, laughing.

"Okay."

Chris started the car again and finished the drive in a better mood. He seized her as soon as they entered the house.

"You scared me," he said, pulling her into his arms.

"How?"

"I thought you were having doubts about . . . you know, us."

"I wasn't."

"I don't ever want to see you looking at me like that again."

"You won't. Forget about it." She kissed him repeatedly, distracting him until he picked her up and set her on the sofa.

"Here?" she said.

"Why not? Are you expecting a visitor?" He grabbed her T-shirt by its hem and pulled it over her head.

"I love this creamy skin right here," he said, bending to kiss the tops of her breasts where the flesh swelled above her bra.

Helene sighed and lay back against his arm.

"And here," he added, moving his lips to the base of her throat. She ran her fingers through his thick hair as he unhooked her bra deftly with one hand and the scrap of lace fell to the floor.

"I used to have dreams about you making love to me," she said softly, stretching out on the couch as he pressed her back with the palm of his hand against her bare shoulder.

"So did I. I had the first one the night I met you." He unzipped her jeans, pulled them off her legs and tossed them onto the floor.

"That fast?"

"That fast." He knelt next to her on the rug and pressed his cheek to her thigh, his eyes closed.

"I remember what I thought when I first saw you," she said, looking down at him.

He opened his eyes, "What?"

"You were half naked, if you recall, and I thought you had a beautiful body."

He grunted, running his hand deliberately over the satiny surface of her other leg.

"I couldn't get you out of my mind," she said, sighing as he moved his hand and placed his splayed fingers on her belly, just above the line of her pants.

"Did you try?" he asked.

"Yes."

"I guess you weren't too successful." He smiled and hooked his index finger under the waistband of her briefs.

"Do you believe that some things were just meant to be?" she asked, noticing the sheen of the lamplight on his bent head.

"Like fate?" he said, tugging.

"Yes."

"Lift," he said, and she raised her hips. He pulled her briefs off and tossed them over his shoulder, where they caught, swinging, on the umbrella stand near the door.

"You didn't answer my question," Helene said, as he sat back and began to unbutton his shirt.

"Well," he replied, considering, "something sure sent you my way, and if you want to call it fate that's all right with me." He shrugged off his shirt and unbuckled his belt.

"Are you glad?" she asked, watching him undress.

"Are you kidding?" he countered, looming above her.

She hooked her arms around his neck and drew him down to her. "I mean it, Chris," she said. "I know I rocked your world. Sometimes you even seem to resent how much you feel for me and the power you feel it gives me."

"You think too much," he said, twining his limbs with hers and kissing the tip of her nose. "If I resent anything, it's the time I wasted before I found you."

"But..." she began.

"Shut up," he said, and kissed her quiet.

Ten days later they came in from a shopping trip and found a box sitting in the middle of the kitchen table.

"What's this?" Helene asked, pushing aside a stack of partially opened mail to pick it up and rattle it. "It's heavy."

"Maria must have left it here," Chris mused, glancing briefly at the shipping label.

"You know what it is?"

"Certainly. It's a baby saddle."

"A baby saddle? Don't you think you're jumping the gun a little bit, Dad?"

"It pays to be prepared," he said sagely

"I'm sure it does, but Mom is going to announce when junior is ready for riding lessons. The saddle will not be in use a moment before that, agreed?"

"Agreed."

Helene kissed him. "Come to bed," she said.

"I'll be right in. I just want to check the mail," he replied.

She nodded and went ahead. She had undressed and was waiting for him in bed when he came through the door, a sheaf of papers in his hand.

"Did you write a letter to your school district asking for your job back next year?" he said accusingly.

She sat up. "Wait..." she began.

"And what's this?" he went on, interrupting her. "A letter from my lawyer outlining your alimony and child-support expectations. I guess my fight with Randy had more of an impact than you admit. Just when were you planning to divorce me?''

Eight

Helene stared at him. His thunderous expression assured her that he wasn't kidding.

"Will you let me explain?" she finally said.

He said nothing, his eyes narrowed and flinty.

"I wrote that letter to the school board three weeks ago, when you weren't even speaking to me."

"So? You didn't cancel it."

"I wasn't even thinking about it!" she said in exasperation. "When I left on leave I was given a deadline to advise the board about next year—I had to write when I did. After we got together it just went out of my mind. It wasn't important anymore."

"And this?" he demanded, waving the envelope with the legal letterhead engraved on its corner.

"He wrote to me, Christopher, after a discussion *you* had with him. I had no idea it was coming—you must have told him you wanted an outline of your obligations sent to me some time ago. I meant to mention it to you tonight, but I forgot about it."

"I don't believe you," he said flatly.

Helene was stunned. "What?" she eventually managed, her voice barely audible.

"You've been planning to dump me once you have the baby."

Helene sat up straighter, swallowing hard, still unable to comprehend how the relaxed, loving man she'd had dinner with had been transformed into this suspicious, hostile stranger so quickly.

"Chris, call the lawyer. Brockman, is that his name?" she said, trying to maintain an air of reasonableness in answering his ridiculous accusations. "He'll tell you I never asked him a thing. You were insisting on alimony and child support. I told you I didn't want it back when you first mentioned it to me. Have you had a memory lapse or something?"

"I can't call Brockman at ten o'clock at night," he said disgustedly, tossing the letters onto the dresser.

"Chris, do you really have to call anybody?" she said quietly, getting out of bed and slipping into his robe.

"What do you mean?" he replied testily, watching her.

"Either you trust me or you don't. I can't go through life defending myself and summoning witnesses every time you have an attack of insecurity."

"I am not insecure!" he exploded, rounding on her furiously.

"No? Apparently you can't believe that I want to stay with you. You keep looking for reasons to think I'm lying about it." She tied the cord of his robe neatly and then faced him squarely, feigning a calmness she did not feel.

"Your degree is in education, isn't it? I'd advise you to stop analyzing me," he said sneeringly.

"You don't have to be a psychiatrist to see what your problem is," she replied.

"I should never have told you about my past life. I knew you would use it against me," he said through clenched teeth, his fists closed, knuckles white.

"Chris," she cried, "I'm not using anything against you. Why can't you accept that I'm on your side? All I'm saying is that you have to abandon this backlog of suspicion and mistrust if there's ever going to be any chance for us."

"Oh," he said in a carefully controlled voice, "is there some doubt of that?"

"You are deliberately misconstruing everything I say," she replied, feeling herself falling in a waking nightmare, slipping and sliding with no way to get a handhold.

"No, I think I'm understanding you very well," he said tightly. "Miss Well Adjusted can't bear the prospect of a future with impossible little old me, isn't that it?"

"I never said that," she answered hopelessly. He was like a runaway train, hurtling out of control. She saw where he was going but was powerless to stop him.

"What, too well-bred to actually *say* it? You're sending the message loud and clear anyway. I guess I'd better remove my offending presence before you call the cops or something." He stormed out of the room and out of the house and seconds later she heard his car starting up on the drive, the motor sounding loud in the night stillness. She listened to the muffled rumble of it fading down the drive as her heartbeat slowly returned to normal.

It was over so quickly that once he was gone she could hardly believe that the quarrel had happened. But the crumpled stationery on the dresser and her empty bed were mute witnesses to the event.

Chris didn't come back to the house that night. In the morning Sam told her that Chris had gone to a horse auction in Red Pass, about forty miles away, and would be returning on Thursday. Unable to bear Sam's quietly sympathetic expression, which spoke volumes, Helene merely nodded and turned away without reply.

As soon as Maria arrived she knew that something was wrong. She sat in stunned silence at the kitchen table as Helene recounted the fight, concluding with a description of Chris's dramatic exit from the house the previous night.

"And I haven't heard anything since then," Helene added, sighing heavily. "Sam said that he went to a horse auction and maybe he did, but I'm sure it's also a convenient excuse to avoid me." She bit her lip. "Maria, I'm not sure how much more of this I can take. Every time I think he finally trusts me something like this happens. It's as if he can't let himself go that final distance. At the last minute he finds some excuse like this ridiculous fight to pull back and run headlong in the other direction. I feel like I'm walking a tightrope every minute. I never know who or what will set him off."

"Dios mio," Maria muttered, putting her hand over Helene's on the table.

"What do you suggest?"

Maria shook her head helplessly.

"Thanks a lot. I thought you were supposed to be the expert," Helene said despairingly.

"I really believed that he was past all that. He seemed so happy," Maria replied.

"I believed it too."

"Maybe when he comes back you can talk to him...." Maria began hopefully.

"And start that whole miserable cycle all over again?" Helene interrupted, reading her mind. "I feel like a yo-yo being pulled this way and that, bobbing around just waiting for the next violent yank in another direction. It's maddening."

"I know he loves you."

"Unfortunately that doesn't mean he trusts me."

"The two usually go together."

"Not in this case. And I don't know if they ever will."

"It's not fair to expect him to change overnight," Maria said in a conciliatory tone.

"I've told myself that a hundred times."

"You're not going to give up on him, are you?" Maria asked, alarmed at her tone.

"I haven't made any decisions. I don't know how I can live like this, but when I think of life without him..." She let the sentence trail off into silence.

"Wait until he gets back. You'll make it up with him."

Helene was silent. She wasn't so sure.

The pains began on Wednesday, the afternoon before Chris was due to return. Maria was polishing silverware in the kitchen when she heard Helene calling her from the bedroom.

"What is it?" she responded breathlessly, her expression changing when reached the doorway and saw Helene doubled up on the bed.

"Call the doctor. Something is wrong," Helene gasped. "I have such terrible cramps and there's blood...."

Maria flew to the phone and returned minutes later to cover Helene with a blanket and grab her hand.

"Hold on," Maria said soothingly. "The ambulance is on the way. Dr. Stern is going to meet us at the hospital. Just try to take it easy, try to relax.

"I can't lose the baby," Helene moaned.

"No, no, none of that," Maria shushed her. "Don't talk, don't even think. Conserve your strength."

Then they both heard the wail of the siren coming up the drive.

The first person Helene saw when she opened her eyes was Dr. Stern. She knew by the expression on his face what had happened.

"Oh, no," she whispered and turned away from him, her eyes filling with tears.

He patted her hand. "These things happen, especially with a first baby," he said. "It may not mean much to you now, but I promise you that you can have other children and you can start trying as soon as you recover."

"My fault," she moaned.

"Now I don't want to hear that," he said firmly. "You did nothing wrong. I was worried about this pregnancy all along—you know that. But each one is different and next time you may have no trouble at all."

Next time, Helene thought in a drugged daze. What was he talking about? What next time?

Maria's worried face appeared in the background. "Just a few minutes. She needs to rest," Dr. Stern said warningly and nodded at the hovering nurse to make sure she enforced his orders.

"*Pobre niña,*" Maria said, sitting next to her bed.

"Chris," Helene murmured.

"What about him?"

"Does he know?"

Maria hesitated, then shook her head. "I haven't talked to him. He hasn't called the house. He's supposed to be back today, isn't he?"

"Is it Thursday?"

Maria nodded.

"Yes, today."

"Do you want me to tell him?"

Helene closed her eyes and two tears seeped from under her lids and trailed slowly down her cheeks.

"I guess you might as well," she mumbled finally.

"I think that's enough," the nurse said sternly.

Maria rose to go. "I'll be back tonight," she said in parting.

Helene nodded and closed her eyes again, glad to return to the oblivion of sleep.

When Helene woke again it was Friday and she felt clearheaded for the first time since she had lost the baby.

"Oh, you're awake," a different nurse said. "Too bad you missed your husband. You were asleep when he was here."

"When was that?"

"Last night. He came in as soon as he heard what happened. He was away, wasn't he?"

Helene nodded wordlessly.

The nurse lowered her tone. "Very broken up he was, too. The doctor sent him home because he was afraid he would upset you."

"Doesn't matter," Helene said tonelessly.

"What?"

"Nothing. Nothing matters."

"Oh, here's your friend," the nurse said brightly, glad of an excuse to escape Helene's depressing presence.

Maria sat next to the bed and waited until the nurse had left before she said, "I told him."

Helene looked at her.

"He was wild, *niña*. I've never seen him like that. Crying, blaming himself."

"There's a lot of that going around."

"He thinks all of this is his fault because of the fight."

"I had the miscarriage four days after he left, Maria. Even he can't be in two places at the same time."

"Try to tell him that. Dr. Stern finally threw him out and told him to go home. He wouldn't leave until the doctor threatened to call the police. We had quite a time with him, I can tell you." Her voice dropped. "He's been forbidden to return."

Helene said nothing. She supposed they were fortunate that Chris stopped short of destroying the hospital. She was glad she'd missed the confrontation. She'd had her fill of those for a while.

"Maria, will you do me a favor?" she asked.

"Of course," Maria said.

"Pack me a bag to take with me when I'm discharged. I'm going straight back to New Jersey. You can send the rest of my things on after me."

There was a protracted silence while Maria debated what to say. She didn't wanted to argue with a hospitalized woman, but it was clear that she disagreed with Helene's decision.

"Are you sure you want to do that?" Maria ventured finally, abandoning neutrality.

"Yes."

"You're not even going to see him?"

"What's the point?"

"Are you trying to punish him, Helene?" Maria asked. "It's not necessary, you know. He's doing a good job of punishing himself. You can take my word for that."

"I can't see him, Maria. I've already lost too much. The baby's gone..." she dissolved into silent tears and it was a long moment before she could add "...and seeing Chris would just remind me."

"Of what?"

"Of how much I love him and how hopeless it all is."

"He'd come here in a minute, no matter what Dr. Stern says, if he thought you wanted to see him."

Helene shook her head, unable to speak.

"All right," Maria said soothingly. "Don't cry. I'll do as you say, don't worry."

"I have no strength left," Helene managed to whisper, wiping her eyes helplessly.

"You'll get it back."

"I won't get my baby back."

Maria patted her hand, tears welling up in her own eyes.

"Or Chris," Helene added mournfully.

"Oh, *niña,* you can have him."

Helene shook her head. "I can't, I never did. It was a dream. I'm awake now."

Maria didn't know what to say.

"When are they discharging me?" Helene asked.

"Dr. Stern says day after tomorrow."

"So you'll bring me the bag then?"

"Yes."

"I'll arrange for a flight and a taxi as soon as they get me a phone. The nurse said she had ordered one for me, but everything takes an eternity here."

"I'll go and check on it," Maria said and walked out of the room to the nurses' station.

Chris was waiting anxiously in the kitchen when Maria came through the back door at the Homestead.

Maria looked at him and shook her head.

Chris closed his eyes and hung his head. "I knew it. She won't see me."

"No."

"She blames me," he said tonelessly.

"No, Chris, she's just...exhausted. You can't imagine what it's like to lose a child. The feeling of emptiness is just overwhelming. I had two miscarriages and I've never forgotten that feeling. You get over it, but you never, ever forget."

"It's me," he said, his voice breaking. He slumped back against the wall, his eyes still closed. "I upset her by picking that fight and then running out on her, she knows that. That's why she had the miscarriage. She won't forgive me."

"Please, stop this," Maria said sharply, setting her purse on the kitchen table. "I'm so tired of listening to the both of you tearing at your wounds."

"When is she getting out of the hospital?"

"Soon, but..."

"What?" he said, his eyes flying open, alarmed at the change in her voice.

"She's going right back to New Jersey."

"She doesn't want to see me ever again?" he said, trying to absorb the enormity of it.

"Don't be silly, just not this minute. In time she will realize that this isn't the end of the world. She can have other babies..."

"Not my babies," he said huskily. "She wouldn't want my babies, not now."

"You can't know that."

"I know," he insisted miserably. "Oh, God, if I could just take it all back...."

"It wouldn't make any difference, Chris. Things like this are out of our hands."

"She'll divorce me now," he said hopelessly.

Maria said nothing. She knew that Helene loved Chris, but in her current frame of mind she might do just that.

"Let me make you some dinner," Maria suggested, to change the subject.

"I'm not hungry."

"You haven't eaten a meal since this happened. You'll have something now," Maria said firmly, putting on her apron. "Sit down there and I'll get you an omelet, at least."

He obeyed woodenly, as if too dispirited to argue.

Maria bustled around the kitchen, falling into her familiar routine, providing the only comfort she could offer.

When she looked back at him he was sitting with his head buried in his folded arms.

Helene looked around at the furniture in her apartment. Everything seemed unreal—the furniture preserved under a light layer of dust, the plants, watered by a neighbor, already drooping after a thirst of several days. The plane flight had passed in a blur of plastic snacks and stewardess's inquiries. She hardly remembered it or the ride back here. She had called Maria and her mother upon arrival and now there was nothing left to do but sprawl on her bed, so long unused, and contemplate her dubious future.

Maybe she could go back to work full-time in January. It would help to have something to do. The months stretched ahead of her like an endless empty canvas: no baby, no Christopher, no job. She felt the tears beginning again and forced them back with an effort of will. No more crying. She had done enough of that for a lifetime.

She got up on slightly wobbly legs and went into her tiny kitchenette to make a cup of tea.

As soon as Helene felt up to it, about a month after her return to New Jersey, she went to Martin's former law partner, Jim Kerry, to talk to him about the divorce. She told him she wanted nothing except a final decree, but once he wrote to Brockman the answer came back that Chris insisted upon contributing alimony.

Helene heard this response with a mental sigh. She should have remembered his pride; he would not let her get away without this reminder of their time together.

"I don't want it," she said to Kerry, as they sat in his office one day in late October.

"Well, your husband is being difficult and if you fight him on this it could delay the whole proceeding. My understanding was that you wanted this over with as quickly as possible."

Helene heard the warning in his voice. "What do you suggest?" she said wearily.

"First, I always tell a woman in your situation to take the money—you never know what the future might hold. It's just sound advice, legally. Second, I think you should meet with your husband to talk this over. It would be easier to work out the terms face-to-face instead of trying to do it through the mail."

"No," she said.

"No?" Kerry echoed, one eyebrow raised. "Is there some animosity involved? Are you afraid of him?"

Not in the way you mean, Helene thought. "No," she said aloud, "that's not it."

"I had understood that this was a marriage of convenience to Martin's brother because of the child. But now that the pregnancy is . . . terminated . . . you want a divorce, isn't that correct?"

"Yes," she said shortly. Terminated. What a word.

"Then I think you should see him. Brockman says here in his letter that your husband will come to this office any time to address this. Should I arrange it?"

Helene was silent.

Kerry waited expectantly.

"All right," she said finally, rising and shouldering her purse. "Let me know the time."

She walked out of the office as Kerry stared after her, his expression thoughtful.

It was the day before Halloween, a blustery autumn afternoon, when Helene walked up the interior staircase of Kerry's office building to his suite. She had been here many times with Martin, but since she had been coming to this place in connection with her divorce, the very carpets and pictures and plaques seemed different, alien. She had taken special care with her appearance, selecting a peach wool two-piece dress to wear with a new pair of pumps. She thought she was ready, but nothing could really prepare her for her first sight of Chris in close to six weeks. Her heart was beating rapidly and her mouth was dry as she opened the door to Kerry's office and saw Chris sitting in the waiting room, alone.

He stood as he saw her and their eyes met. Helene thought immediately that he looked thinner, but it made him even more handsome, giving his cheekbones more prominence and accentuating the planes of his face. He was wearing an eggshell sweater with a tan checked jacket and brown twill slacks. He seemed too big for the office, too tanned and fit to be confined by four paneled walls. Had she forgotten how black his hair was, how firm and sculptured his mouth? Why couldn't the man ever look bad? she wondered desperately. His undimmed allure wouldn't make dealing with him any easier.

"Hello, Helene," he said, in the husky, haunting voice she heard nightly in her dreams.

"Hello, Chris."

"You look terrific," he said.

What a liar he was. She hadn't slept for two nights running in anticipation of seeing him and she probably looked like Mina Von Helsing after a visit from Dracula.

"Thank you. I'm feeling better."

"Are you working?"

"I'm substitute teaching on a day-to-day basis. I hope to get something more permanent after the holidays." She paused. "How is the ranch?"

"Fine. I left Sam in charge." He coughed nervously. "We bought three new Arabians last week."

"That's good."

"Maria tells me you write to her all the time."

"Yes, I miss her." Was it possible that they were standing in this sanitized cubicle exchanging pleasantries as if they were former classmates meeting at old home week? She felt as if she were watching herself in a movie.

"Mr. Kerry will see you now, Mr. and Mrs. Murdock," the receptionist announced behind them.

They filed in together and took seats across from Kerry's broad desk, which was littered with files. His phone had several lines, two of which were glowing.

Kerry got up briskly and shook hands with Chris after nodding to Helene.

"Nice to meet you, Murdock. Martin always spoke well of you. We really miss him around here, I can tell you." He glanced past Chris into the hall. "Brockman didn't come with you?" he added, sitting again in his leather chair.

"I don't need him. Whatever Helene wants is okay with me. I've already said so," Chris replied.

"I don't want anything," Helene said quickly.

"Now, Helene, don't start that again," Kerry said. "We're having this meeting so that we can agree on a reasonable sum for alimony, and you knew that when you came here."

"I was hoping to change Chris's mind," she said.

"I have to tell you, Helene, you're quite a departure from the divorcing wives I usually encounter in my practice," Kerry said dryly, adjusting the knot of his tie.

"Helene is unusual in a lot of respects," Chris said flatly.

Kerry stared at him for a moment, then cleared his throat as he picked up a file.

"Let's get down to it," he said, "and then I'll call Brockman and see if we can finalize this."

The session was mercifully brief and concluded with Helene agreeing to accept a minimal sum just to end the agony of enduring Chris's presence next to her. As they were leaving Kerry said jovially, "I wish all the couples I saw were as reasonable as you two. In fact, I'm having a little trouble understanding why you're divorcing at all."

The silence was deafening.

"So," Kerry said, to break it, "Chris, how long are you staying in town?"

"I don't know yet."

"Can I arrange to drop you somewhere, your hotel or anything, the airport?"

"No, thanks, I can handle it," Chris replied.

"Well, nice meeting you," Kerry concluded. "If there's anything else I can do, just let me know."

"I will."

The two men shook hands and then the lawyer hurried back into his office.

His farewell left them standing awkwardly in the waiting room. Helene glanced over at the receptionist, typing away behind her glass screen, headphones in place. The woman looked up and smiled pleasantly, obviously wondering why they were lingering when their business was done.

"I have to go," Helene said suddenly, bolting into the hall.

Chris dashed out after her.

"Are you really going to just go away and leave me?" he said.

Nine

"Chris, please don't do this," Helene said, continuing to flee down the hall.

"Do what? I just want to talk to you."

"There's nothing to say."

"Do you want it to end this way, in a lawyer's office?" he asked, moving ahead to block her path.

"It has to end some way. We've hurt each other enough."

He jammed his hands in his pockets, taking a breath. "Helene, I'm sorry about the baby."

She looked away. "I know you are."

"It was our last link to Martin, a loss for both of us."

She nodded.

"They wouldn't let me see you at the hospital."

"Maria told me. Let's not go over it again, Chris, it's too painful and I'm trying to forget it."

"Me too? Are you trying to forget me too?" He put his hand on her arm, a muscle in his jaw working.

"I can't do that," she whispered.

"But you'd like to?"

"It would be easier."

He released her. "Easier," he said.

"Yes."

"All right," he said tonelessly. "Brockman will take care of the legal stuff. Goodbye."

"Goodbye," she said through a mist of tears, and dashed ahead for the stairs.

By the time she reached the landing she was crying.

Chris watched her go, every instinct he had screaming at him to run after her. But he stayed right where he was. Of course, she wanted to be rid of him; of course, she wanted to forget him. What else had he expected? Did he think she would take one look at him and throw herself into his arms?

Well, he had hoped. Obviously she hadn't missed him as much as he had missed her. Or she was tougher than he had guessed—Chris had a sinking feeling it was the latter. He had an extremely refined self-protective urge himself where emotions were concerned, born of long years of childhood misery. But he was learning that it could be a curse as well as an advantage. It had caused him to doubt Helene, and her experience with him was now causing her to run away from him lest her well-remembered pain return.

God, the look on her face when she saw him, the longing battling with the fortified defenses. Her every thought was mirrored on her face. She might still want him, but her will to resist was stronger than her desire to submit, and he knew he had taught her that—to hold back and consider. He had turned her into the frightened and defensive woman he had met today.

He sat down on the top step of the staircase, rubbing his eyes. It was over. There was nothing left but to go home. He had missed his chance for happiness; his future would be nothing but a catalog of regrets. He bent his head and despair overwhelmed him.

A couple came through the lower door and he stood abruptly, turning away so they wouldn't see his face. There was a bank of public phones to his left and he walked toward it, intending to call a taxi to take him to the airport.

Looking for a distraction, Helene stopped off at the condo to check on her mother and sister, chatting with them about everyday things while dying inside. The day darkened during the afternoon and as she left it started to rain, the weather reflecting her spirits perfectly. She drove back to her apartment in the secondhand car she'd bought during her first year of teaching and parked in the lot of the complex. She held her coat over her head as she dashed for the door.

Inside, sitting on the floor in front of her apartment, his elbows propped on his knees, was Chris.

He got up when he saw her and she stood stock-still, trying to absorb the fact that he wasn't on a plane but standing in front of her.

"I couldn't go back without you," he said simply.

Helene was speechless.

"Will you let me come inside and talk to you?" he asked.

Helene fumbled for her key and dropped it.

Chris picked it up off the floor and unlocked her door, holding it open for her. She walked past him in a daze and then he followed her into the apartment.

"May I sit?" he asked.

Helene nodded, marveling at his Sunday school behavior. Was this the same man who had hired an investigator to dig up dirt about her?

He took off his jacket and dropped it on her reclining chair. Helene noticed that his hands were shaking. He was not as controlled as he appeared.

He sat on her sofa, leaning forward with his hands clasped, staring at the floor. "I've gone over this in my mind a thousand times, what to say, how to say it," he began. "I don't give a damn about alimony or any of that legal mumbo jumbo. I think you know that. I came here today because it was an excuse to see you and for six weeks I haven't been able to work up the nerve to do that on my own."

Helene listened, incredulous. Chris Murdock, lacking nerve? Impossible.

"I know I have no right to ask, after the way I treated you, but I don't know what else to do. I can't think of anything but you and how much I miss you."

"Ask what?" Helene said, finding her voice.

"What do I have to do to get you back?" he said huskily, his eyes meeting hers for the first time since he started his speech.

Helene's throat tightened but she didn't say a word.

"Don't you want me anymore?" he asked, defeat and resignation in every line of his body.

"I'll always want you," she said softly.

"But I've driven you away," he said.

She didn't answer.

"I never meant to do that," he said quietly. "I was just so scared that you would leave me."

"Why?" she said. "Why did you think I would leave when it was so clear that I loved you?"

"It wasn't clear," he said.

She was stunned. "What do you mean?"

"You had a physical thing for me, but I've had that before..." He let it hang, but she knew what he meant.

"You thought I was just infatuated with you?" she asked.

"Sometimes. It was all new for you—I thought you might be confused."

"And when the infatuation wore off, when desire tempered and I saw what a rat you really were, then of course I would pack my bags. Is that it?"

"Something like that," he murmured.

"You don't give me much credit," she said softly.

"I guess not."

"Why not?"

He thought a long time before he answered. "It was too good to be true. Things like that don't happen to me."

"It did."

He shrugged. "I couldn't trust it."

"Or me."

He got up and came to her side, looking down at her with the heavily lashed eyes she hadn't been able to forget.

"Please give me another chance," he said simply. "I can't promise that I'll reform overnight, but I'll try my best to be everything you want me to be. I'll never make you sorry you took me back."

Helene put her arms around his neck and rested her head against his shoulder. "I love you," she said quietly.

She felt the tension leave his body and he bent to press his cheek to her hair.

"You'll never be sorry," he said again, choking on the last word, holding her so tightly she could barely breathe.

They stood that way for a long moment and then he turned her face up to kiss her.

"I missed you so much," he said against her mouth.

"You don't have to miss me anymore," she replied.

"Is that the bedroom?" he said, pointing to the closed door behind them.

"That's it."

He picked her up without comment and she turned the door handle as they went through it. He set her on the bed and began to take off her clothes.

"I thought I'd never make love to you again," he said shakily, bungling his attempt to unfasten her blouse.

"Let me do it," she said and discarded her top and skirt.

He seized her and bore her back down on the bed before she could finish undressing.

"I can handle the rest," he said, and he did. He was hungry, wild, kissing each part of her body as he uncovered it, pausing only to strip quickly and join her again. He entered her as soon as she embraced him and she arched her back to meet him, sobbing.

"Don't cry," he whispered, pulling her close.

"I'm so happy," she replied.

"You'll always be happy from now on. I mean it," he said, and she believed him.

An hour later they were curled up on her bed like two puppies napping in a basket, enjoying the sensation of closeness they had both missed so sorely.

"This is a nice apartment," he said suddenly.

"You just noticed that?" she replied teasingly.

"I mean, the colors go together and everything. It looks good. I guess women are better at that stuff than men."

"Is that a reference to Ginny Porter?"

"Well, she had a nice place too," he said dryly.

"How is dear old Ginny?"

"She moved to Las Vegas two weeks after you left."

"But not before she gave you the old college try one last time, correct?"

"She didn't get anywhere. I haven't been with a woman since you came back here."

"That's comforting."

"I couldn't think about anybody else but you. And of course I had other problems once I put that guy in a cast...." he said.

Helene sat up. "What guy?" she said in a strong voice.

He looked at her. "Maria didn't tell you?"

"No, it seems she skipped the best part."

"I guess she didn't want to upset you."

"What happened?"

"Well, when they wouldn't let me see you at the hospital, I put up a fight."

"Why am I not surprised?"

"The security guard who tried to stop me—I hit him."

"And?"

"I broke his jaw. And his wrist."

"Oh, Chris."

"I didn't meant to. Everything just got out of hand. Actually, I only broke his jaw with a punch—he broke his wrist when he fell."

"Gee, that makes a big difference."

"And now he's suing me," he added glumly.

Helene couldn't help it. She started to giggle.

"It isn't funny," he said darkly.

"What is he suing you for?"

"Assault or something, I don't know. Brockman says I have to write him a letter apologizing and offering a monetary settlement. That will most likely keep it out of court."

"Brockman could retire on your business alone."

"I'd like to go into court and explain the situation. I'd probably get off scot-free."

"Don't count on it. Most people don't think violence is an appropriate reaction to stress."

He traced the line of her collarbone with his finger. "I promise I'll do better."

"You'll have to, Chris, or we'll never be able to afford the legal bills."

"Just think of the money we'll be saving by skipping the divorce," he said, grinning.

She shot him a look and his grin widened.

"Speaking of that," he said, "do you still have the wedding ring I gave you?"

"Of course. Did you think I hocked it?"

"You're not wearing it."

"Up until a couple of hours ago, my dear, I was sure I wouldn't need it."

"Now you will. Let's have a big wedding as soon as possible, in church with a reception—the works. Maria can be matron of honor, she'll get a kick out of that."

"We'll see. I have to think about it."

He fell across her in mock despair. "Oh, no, she's thinking again," he said dramatically.

"Not for long," she replied, bending to kiss the back of his neck.

"Are you starting something?" he asked, turning to embrace her again.

"I certainly hope so."

"Then I'll finish it," he said.

And he did.

Epilogue

———

"Martin, what do you have behind your back?" Helene asked patiently, watching the toddler closely.

He presented her with an expression as innocent and angelic as that of a Botticelli Madonna.

"Show me," she said.

He shook his head.

Helene sighed. "We don't want to bother Daddy with this when he comes in, do we? He has other things on his mind today."

Martin considered that for a long moment, then thrust his fist forward, still clenched.

"Open," she said.

His fingers relaxed.

"Bug," he announced.

"Yes, indeed, that is a bug," Helene said, wrinkling her nose as she examined the rather large, very dead bee. The insect was cradled in the palm of the child's hand on its back, multiple legs curled upward in final surrender.

"May I have it?" she asked.

"Mine," Martin said stubbornly.

One look into his brown eyes, so like his father's, convinced her that a contest of wills was about to ensue.

"Gee, I wonder if Maria made that lemonade she promised you," Helene said brightly, shamelessly employing a diversionary tactic. "Do you think it's ready?"

He glanced toward the house.

"I know what. Why don't you leave the bee here with me while you get your drink and then you can pick him up later?"

"Okay." He handed her his inanimate prize and went over to the door, pressing his nose to the screen. Helene tossed the bee carcass into the grass as she watched Maria admit him to the house. She wondered how long she would be able to outwit him—he was, after all, not yet two. It didn't bode well for the future that he was presenting a challenge already.

"Any for you?" Maria called from the doorway, holding up a plastic pitcher.

"No, thanks."

"I've started dinner," Maria added.

"I'm coming in," Helene replied, shifting her lesson plans off her lap and setting them on the picnic table. She was teaching Martin's preschool class on Saturday morning and she was two weeks behind in her scheduling. Oh, well. It would have to wait. She went up the back steps and into the house.

Martin was sitting at the kitchen table, kicking his legs and sipping from a glass decorated with cartoon characters. Maria was at the stove, checking the roast in the oven and simultaneously stirring the contents of a pot.

"Ah, there you are," Maria said, putting down her spoon and untying her apron briskly. "Turn this oven off in ten minutes and I'm going to cover the pot and reduce the heat. The tomatoes should be ready in about half an hour."

Helene nodded. "Thanks."

"More," Martin said, extending his empty glass.

"No more," Helene replied.

"More," Martin said again, waving the glass imperiously.

"That's full of sugar, young man. One glass is quite enough," Helene said sternly.

"Cookie," Martin said.

Maria chuckled under her breath.

"Don't encourage him." To her son she said, "I think you're missing the point, boy of mine. No more lemonade, no cookies, no goodies of any kind. We're having dinner just as soon as your father gets here."

"Bug," he said, looking at her.

"Oh, dear, I was really hoping he'd forgotten about that," Helene sighed.

"What?" Maria said, picking up her purse.

"He found a dead bee in the yard."

"Where is it?"

"I threw it away and now he wants it back."

"Good luck," Maria said, grinning.

"Why doesn't he play with trains or something?" Helene said despairingly. "He's always finding things outside and bringing them in, rocks and shells and plants—once it was a discarded skin some snake had shed." She shuddered.

"Maybe he'll be one of those scientists who classifies things."

"Good, then he can pay for my psychiatric care. If he hands me one more grisly object I will go mad."

"You're just not used to little boys." Maria slipped into her sweater and ruffled Martin's hair affectionately. "He has a fine, curious mind. Don't you, sweetheart?"

Martin grinned up at her, displaying a perfect set of baby teeth, rows of tiny pearls.

"You spoil him," Helene chided her.

"Of course, that's what godmothers are for," Maria replied, winking as she passed the table. "I'll see you on Friday," she called in farewell, pulling the door closed behind her.

"Maria's gone," Martin announced.

"Yes, but she'll be back. Now let's hiphop like a bunny and wash your hands so you'll be ready for dinner."

"Bug," he said.

"Buster, the bug is outside, where he will remain. We'll look for him tomorrow. Come on."

He slipped off the chair and took her hand as they walked down the hall. Helene felt a surge of tenderness for him, for the little fingers placed so trustingly in hers, for the cowlick growing at the part in his hair, exactly where Chris had one. It was hard to imagine that in fifteen years he would undoubtedly be breaking hearts, just like his father. Right now he seemed so small.

When they reached the bathroom he pushed his stool into position so he could reach the taps and turned them on, testing the temperature. Helene handed him a bar of soap and watched as he lathered industriously, the water turning brackish as it ran off his hands. She sighed mentally. No matter how many times she bathed him, he was always filthy.

They both heard the door slam and Martin dropped the soap immediately, scrambling off the stool.

"Daddy!" he screamed, lurching into the doorway.

"Where's my boy?" Chris called back. Helene stepped into the hall in time to see Chris scoop the squirming child into his arms and swing him in a circle. Martin chortled appreciatively as Chris tickled him and then set him down.

"And there's my gorgeous wife," Chris said, spying her and extending his arm. Helene fitted herself into its curve and rested her head on his shoulder.

"Has my son been behaving himself?" Chris asked.

"No," Helene replied, laughing.

"What?" Chris said, feigning surprise.

"Now he's collecting bees," she said in an under-tone.

"Collecting?"

"Well, actually it was only one and it was dead, but I fear the beginning of a trend."

"Bug," Martin said delightedly, tugging on Chris's jeans.

"See?" Helene said darkly.

"He's a botanist!" Chris declared, picking the child up again.

"That's plants, Chris."

"A natural historian, then. A genius of some kind, that's certain. And now, wonder boy, let's see what Mom's got cooking for our dinner."

Helene trailed after them, shaking her head, as Chris carried Martin into the kitchen.

"Time for bed," Helene announced, as she finished buttoning her son's pajamas. They were both dressed for bed, but Martin was pulling his usual delaying tactics.

"Time for story," Martin countered, grinning slyly.

"All right, just one."

"Sad little pony," the child announced, pointing to the bookshelf beside his bed.

"Okay, go get it."

Martin retrieved his favorite book and settled himself on the bed as Helene resigned herself to yet another reading of the same story. He never seemed to tire of hearing about the "sad little, bad little" pony, who couldn't be trained and was always in trouble. Helene was afraid it was because he identified with it.

"There once was a sad little pony," she began, turning the well-worn page as she talked. The book was falling apart, the binding a mass of desiccated glue, but Martin refused a replacement. He was attached to this particular copy, as well as the story, which featured his two great loves, horses and dogs. His lips moved along with hers as she read; he had the text memorized.

"Again," he said, when she finished.

"Martin, Daddy will be back with Rover any minute now. We don't have time."

Chris had gone to pick up their dog from the vet's. As if in response to her statement, the car pulled into the drive.

"Rover!" Martin said excitedly, forgetting the book.

The door slammed and they heard snuffling and the patter of wildly scampering paws as Rover, a black cocker spaniel puppy with a white splash on his chest, came flying down the hall. He shot through the air and landed on Martin, who was screaming with laughter. The dog smothered the boy with loud, wet kisses.

"Well, I must say Rover seems none the worse for wear," Helene said dryly to Chris, who was lounging in the doorway, grinning at the spectacle on the bed.

"Dr. Bock gave him a shot for the infected ear," Chris replied. "And he had a chicken fajita at Super Burger on the way home."

"Christopher, how many times have I told you not to give that dog Mexican food?" Helene said in strong voice.

"He likes it."

"He won't eat his dog chow tomorrow. And when he doesn't, I'll just send you out for a special order of tacos, okay?"

Chris ambled over and kissed her lingeringly on the side of her throat. "Okay, *mamacita*," he said in a chastened voice, which didn't fool her for a minute.

Rover shot off the bed and began to rocket around the room, panting madly. Martin shouted encouragement from the bed, waving his arms and giggling.

"I guess Rover's excited to be home," Chris said, laughing.

"Well, at least he saved me from three renditions of the bad little pony," Helene replied dryly, sneaking the book back onto the shelf while Martin was preoccupied with the dog.

"Okay, buddy," Chris announced to his son, "Rover has to go back to his bed in the kitchen."

Rover chose that moment to vault onto the bed and land on his back at Martin's feet, paws in the air. Martin looked up at them with mute appeal flooding his huge brown eyes and pleaded, "Rover stay with me?"

Helene groaned.

"That's up to your mother, kiddo," Chris said, taking the coward's way out.

"Chris, the bed will be full of fleas by morning," Helene said in an undertone.

"Are you suggesting that Rover has fleas?" Chris asked in mock horror.

"Please?" Martin said, adopting a perfect imitation of his father's most beguiling expression. To add to the pitiful tableau, Rover whimpered adoringly and thumped his tail once.

"I give up," Helene said, shrugging and throwing out her hands in resignation.

Martin yodeled and hugged the dog, who licked his face enthusiastically.

"Just this once," she added, trying to hang on to some semblance of discipline.

"Now lights out," Chris said.

"Pillow for Rover?" Martin suggested.

"Don't push your luck, kid," Chris advised him, switching off the lamp next to the bed and turning on the night-light. As if in response to some secret signal, Rover flopped onto his side at the foot of the bed and sighed deeply.

"I know I'm going to regret this," Helene said. "He'll have Stomper sleeping in here next." Stomper was Martin's six-month-old spotted colt.

"G'night, champ," Chris said, bending from the waist to kiss his son's forehead.

"Night, Daddy," the boy said.

Helene tucked him in after Chris left and by the time she closed the bedroom door both boy and dog were deep in dreamland.

"Is he sleeping?" Chris asked as Helene came into their bedroom, yawning.

"Snoring. He's exhausted."

"Come here and join me," Chris said, flipping back the sheet invitingly.

Helene slid in next to him and curled against his warm naked flank, sighing with contentment.

"Do you think he's spoiled?" Chris asked.

"Are you kidding? Of course."

"Is that a problem?"

"If he plans to live among the rest of the human race, it is."

"He'll shape up when he gets to school."

"By the time he gets to school he'll think he's the center of the universe."

Chris was laughing silently; she could feel him shaking.

"It isn't funny," she said.

"I have a solution," he offered.

"I can't wait to hear it."

"Let's have another child."

Helene propped herself up on one elbow and stared down at him.

"Do you mean it?" she said.

"Sure. Let's get started on it this minute," he said, pushing aside the collar of her nightgown with his tongue.

"It's not the right time."

"It's always the right time."

"You know what I mean."

"Then I guess we'll just have to keep working at it until we get it done," he said in mock resignation.

Helene melted into his arms in agreement.

* * * * *

A romantic collection that
will touch your heart....

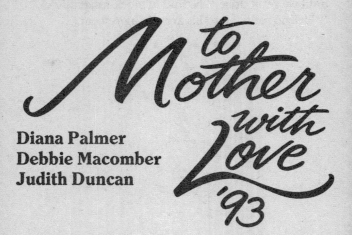

to Mother
with Love
'93

Diana Palmer
Debbie Macomber
Judith Duncan

As part of your annual tribute to
motherhood, join three of Silhouette's
best-loved authors as they celebrate the
joy of one of our most precious gifts—
mothers.

Available in May at your favorite retail outlet.

Only from 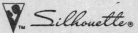 *Silhouette*®

—where passion lives.

Take 4 bestselling love stories FREE

Plus get a FREE surprise gift!

For all those readers who've been looking for something a little bit different, a little bit spooky, let Silhouette Books take you on a journey to the dark side of love with

SILHOUETTE
Shadows™

If you like your romance mixed with a hint of danger, a taste of something eerie and wild, you'll love Shadows. This new line will send a shiver down your spine and make your heart beat faster. It's full of romance and more—and some of your favorite authors will be featured right from the start. Look for our four launch titles wherever books are sold, because you won't want to miss a single one.

THE LAST CAVALIER—Heather Graham Pozzessere
WHO IS DEBORAH?—Elise Title
STRANGER IN THE MIST—Lee Karr
SWAMP SECRETS—Carla Cassidy

After that, look for two books every month, and prepare to tremble with fear—and passion.

SILHOUETTE SHADOWS, coming your way in March.

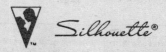

Silhouette®

SHAD1